Bill Knox began his writing career as a young Glasgow journalist and was variously employed as a crime reporter, motoring correspondent and news editor. He made many contributions to radio and television and was well known to Scottish viewers as the writer and presenter for twelve years of the Scottish Television police liaison programme, 'Crime Desk'. Bill Knox died in March 1999.

He wrote twenty-four Thane and Moss books in all as well as many other crime novels and his work has been published in ten languages with world sales in excess of four million copies.

THE DEEP FALL

It was obvious they were dealing with a professional — the killing was vicious and clever. William Carter, managing director of a firm carrying out secret work for the Admiralty, was found dead in his factory's enamelling oven. He left behind him a wide choice of suspects — and the risk of a major security leak. Why had Carter sent urgent messages to his attractive wife and his business partner just before his murder? Had he known that his life was in danger? Thane and Moss, assigned to this most bizarre case, find some of the answers in a booby-trapped building — but the rest of the truth almost comes too late . . .

A Thane and Moss case.

BILL KNOX

◆

THE
DEEP FALL

Complete and Unabridged

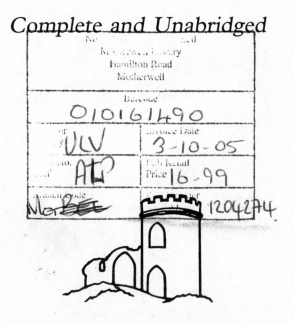

ULVERSCROFT
Leicester

First published in Great Britain in 1966 by
Constable
London

First Large Print Edition
published 2003
by arrangement with
Constable & Robinson Limited
London

British Library CIP Data

Knox, Bill, *1928 – 1999*
    The deep fall.—Large print ed.—
    Ulverscroft large print series: mystery
    1. Thane, Colin (Fictitious character)—Fiction
    2. Detective and mystery stories
    3. Large type books
    I. Title
    823.9'14 [F]

    ISBN 0–7089–4737–9

Published by
F. A. Thorpe (Publishing)
Anstey, Leicestershire
Set by Words & Graphics Ltd.
Anstey, Leicestershire
Printed and bound in Great Britain by
T. J. International Ltd., Padstow, Cornwall

This book is printed on acid-free paper

1

In the world outside the building it was a damp, grey Sunday evening with the wind coming cold from the north. The first street lamps were beginning to glow on deserted, rain-puddled pavements and only the occasional car drove past with a hiss of tyres on wet tarmac. But in the building's world, near its centre, power hummed and vast intakes sucked air, heating, reheating and purifying before thrusting it on into the chamber.

The chamber had walls of clinically white tile. The ceiling was a busy place of fine-meshed ducts and huge heating lamps, glaring down on a floor made up of a network of close-fitting iron gratings, black, ugly but spotlessly clean.

It was hot in the chamber, hot beyond endurance. And it was empty, except for the man. Slowly, despairingly, each muscle's movement an agony of effort, he once more clawed on hands and knees across the gratings towards the single metal-faced door with the ribbon thermometer set high above its centre.

He sobbed as he moved, sobbed with each

tortured breath of the dry, searing heat
... heat which bit and blistered against his
throat and lungs. But he'd stopped shouting,
stopped screaming a long time ago. That took
strength, took effort, and he had none to
spare. He moaned, the sound drowned by the
steady, rasping blast of the air ducts. The heat
in the air dried the perspiration as it flowed
from his body, dried it then demanded more.

At the door, he stopped and raised his
head. Nothing had changed. The thermometer's needle stood steady at its reading.

A small window of armoured glass was set
in the door's surface. His half-crazed brain
registered what might have been a movement
on the other side and his mouth opened wide
in a silent, desperate plea.

But the intakes rasped on, the great battery
of heating lamps glared their constant
torture.

He fell back to the floor, dragged himself
across the gratings to where a scattering of
discarded clothing marked an early stage of
his ordeal, and reached for his jacket. His
hands trembled as he pulled the hot, now
almost brittle cloth over his head in a futile
effort at protection.

The man lay helpless, his fists clenched
tight, his whole body shaking and quivering,
the heat eating greedily into his frame.

And then, at last, it was over. But the heated air still blasted through the filters, the lamps still glared. Another hour passed before a timing clock clicked outside and an electronic circuit was broken. The blast from the intakes died, the bright glow of the lamps faded, and slowly, very slowly, the thermometer's reading began to fall.

★   ★   ★

Small and dapper in a dark coat and stiff white collar, Doc Williams hummed a soft, gentle tune to himself as he worked over the body. Then, sensing an audience, he squatted back on his heels on the metal grating and looked round towards the doorway.

'Morning, Colin.' He cocked his head sideways in bird-like fashion and grinned at the burly, dark-haired figure standing just inside the doorway of the big, white-tiled room. 'Some start to a Monday, eh?'

Chief Detective Inspector Colin Thane, head of Millside Division C.I.D., City of Glasgow Police, stayed where he was, hands deep in the pockets of his tweed sports suit. A young detective constable hovered attentively in the background.

'To a Monday or any other day.' Thane looked first at the battery of heating lamps and air ducts on the ceiling, then down at the body, his broad, rugged face showing a faint wince of distaste. The inside of an industrial enamelling process oven was a hell of a place for anyone to die — and murder made it worse.

'Well, this time I don't mind taking a guess on the post mortem opinion.' Doc Williams stayed in cheerful mood. He'd been a police surgeon in the city for over a decade, long enough to develop a useful, basically protective shell of good humour whatever the circumstances. 'Syncope, Colin — plain heart failure, the result of major heat apoplexy. To spell it out, he was baked to death.'

Thane winced again, more openly, and walked almost reluctantly across the metal gratings. The enamelling oven, one of the latest additions to the factory of Hydrostat Drives Incorporated, was the size of a large bedroom. The dead man lay as he'd been found, about five yards in from the doorway, but with the jacket removed from around his head. He'd been in his mid-thirties, thin-faced, with a long, almost Roman nose. His fair hair was clipped to little more than a crew-cut, a probable attempt to disguise the dome-like effect of a high, prematurely bald forehead.

'There's a touch of cyanosis around the

face, but I'd expect that,' said Doc Williams conversationally. He used one forefinger to scratch the back of his neck. 'You know, it's one of medicine's little oddities that nobody has really worked out why it happens — the heart failure, I mean. But we keep students happy by telling them that great heat deranges the vasometer centres.'

Thane gave a polite grunt. 'What about time of death?'

'In this place?' The police surgeon sucked his teeth, a sure sign of a negative answer. 'Not a hope. The heat that would be generated throws every possible body temperature calculation straight out of the nearest window, and does the same for rigor and the rest. If we're lucky, I'll be able to give you a rough approximation to within a few hours — but only once the p.m.'s complete.' He eyed the Millside chief with quizzical concern. 'You've got troubles on this one, Colin.'

With a sigh, Thane glanced at his watch. It was a minute or two before 9 a.m., still less than an hour since the original telephone call had come to Millside Division.

The factory had opened at eight after the weekend break, and the body had been found within a matter of minutes as the enamelling squad prepared for work.

5

There'd been no problem about identification. William Carter, managing director of Hydrostat Drives, had a face well known far beyond the circle of his immediate friends and employees. Until he'd retired from the game a few years back he'd been one of the best amateur running stars ever produced by Britain.

The regular routine went into operation. Detective Sergeant MacLeod was sent out from Millside, Doc Williams was called from his home, the original message was noted in the C.I.D. logbook as a 'query fatal accident.'

But the second telephone call to Millside, made by MacLeod soon after he'd arrived at the plant, changed all that . . . and brought Colin Thane hurrying over at the same time as Headquarters were asked to despatch a Scientific Bureau team.

'You know about the note, Doc?' asked Thane.

'Heard about it, haven't seen it,' said Doc Williams briefly, beginning to ram his scatter of instruments back inside their black leather bag.

Thane turned to the waiting detective constable. 'Find Sergeant MacLeod and ask him to come over.' As the man went off on the errand, he eased his hat back on his forehead. 'You said heat apoplexy, Doc. Isn't

6

that what used to hit stokers in the old coal-fired ships?'

'There's a rough parallel.' The police surgeon snapped his bag shut and rose to his feet. 'The human body can take plenty of punishment and still recover, and some men can work in a temperature that would kill others. But this' — he shook his head — 'how hot did it get in here?'

Thane grimaced. He'd already asked the enamelling squad foreman the same question. 'The control panel was set for a three-hour run at 250 degrees Fahrenheit.'

'That much?' Doc Williams whistled. 'A lot less would have done the job.'

Voices sounded just beyond the door, then Sergeant MacLeod, a bulky, glum-faced figure, walked heavily into the oven chamber.

'Looking for me, sir?'

'The note, Mac,' said Thane softly.

He produced it from an inside pocket, a tiny, crumpled slip of paper now protected by a plastic envelope. Doc Williams handled it with careful, speculative interest.

'Where'd you find it?'

MacLeod showed a trace of grim satisfaction at his own efficiency. 'Jammed inside the strap of his wrist-watch, against the skin.'

Scrawled in pencil, the letters broken and shaky in their outline, the message held its

7

own despairing purpose.

'TRICKED INSIDE. DOOR LOCKED. PLEASE D HELP L — '

There was more, a word which might have been 'get' and three longer, indecipherable pencil strokes tailing off into nothing.

'Well, he tried.' Doc Williams returned the note. 'Pity he couldn't finish it, but most people wait pretty late before they accept they're dying. Any sign of a break-in, Colin?'

'None.'

'His keys seem to be missing,' volunteered MacLeod. 'But the whole plant was locked up when the staff arrived, and he had a wallet with sixty pounds in his hip pocket.'

'People don't kill for that kind of small change any more,' grunted the police surgeon. 'It's one of the minor blessings of the Welfare State. And this part of my job's over. What about the rest, Colin?'

'He'll be moved as soon as the Scientific squad are finished with their stuff,' promised Thane. 'Doc, I think we'd better bring MacMaster in on this one.'

'Hedging your bets?' Doc Williams showed no delight at the prospect. Professor Mac-Master, the elderly, dourly efficient occupant of the Regius chair of forensic medicine at Glasgow University, was by no means his favourite partner in an autopsy room. 'All right, I'll tell him.' He began heading for the door, then stopped. 'I knew there was somebody missing. Where's Phil Moss?'

Thane flickered a grin. Detective Inspector Moss, Millside C.I.D.'s long-suffering second-in-command, had troubles of his own that morning. 'He's having a couple of hours off — personal business.'

'Tell him to give me a call sometime,' said Williams vaguely. 'I want to talk to him. Oh, and if you need me in a hurry, I'll be at the High Court jury trials for the next hour or so. I'm on the witness list — a woman who tried to carve her initials on a boyfriend.'

Thane watched him leave, then stood silent for a moment. The whole set-up in this one troubled him, and other people were going to be more than worried until it was cleared up. Hydrostat Drives Incorporated was one of the names on a confidential Headquarters list he kept locked in his desk, a list devoted exclusively to city firms doing Government contract work with a security classification.

Beyond that, he knew only a little. Hydrostatic drive was something engineering laboratories in half a dozen countries had been playing with for years, a method of using fluid piped under pressure to drive a variety of machines. There had been a vague rumour that the Hydrostat Drives contract was linked with the new sea-to-air missile warships building on the Clyde, but nothing more.

Detective Sergeant MacLeod cleared his throat in diplomatic fashion. 'I've asked around about his next of kin, sir. This 'L' mentioned in the note is probably his wife. Her name's Lynne. But the works manager says she's out of town, probably in London. There's no other family.'

'Which means he wouldn't be missed if he didn't show up at home last night.' Thane glanced at the body on the floor and pursed his lips. 'Mac, how sure are you there's no break-in?'

MacLeod was hurt at the suggestion. 'I've even checked the ruddy roof, sir. There's no night watchman, but the place is wired with alarms every other inch.'

'Where's this works manager?'

'Over in Carter's room, sir, in the office section. His name is Hayston, Peter Hayston.' MacLeod scratched his close-shaven chin. 'I'd say he's pretty shaken up over this, but he's trying to find out if there's anything missing. I told him not to touch anything more than was necessary.'

Thane nodded. 'All right, keep an eye on things here until the Scientific mob arrive. Once they've taken over, start asking the usual questions around the plant — how Carter got on with people, any recent troubles, how he rated as a boss. I'll go and talk to Hayston.'

'Eh . . . have we any special angle, sir?' asked MacLeod hopefully. 'Some of the stuff this place turns out is on the secret list, isn't it?'

'Mac — ' Thane groaned aloud. 'Plenty of people will nudge me in that direction without you starting. Right now there's no angle — except murder.'

★   ★   ★

Hydrostat Drives' entire factory area was contained within one high-roofed two-storey building constructed round a wide central courtyard used mainly as a loading bay and car park. Inside the building, it was easy enough for a stranger to find his way around, thanks to the detailed direction signs placed at each corridor intersection.

From the enamelling section, situated on the ground floor near the rear, Thane threaded his way past a network of small workshops and a larger assembly bay. Most of the machinery was silent, and one glimpse of his tall figure approaching silenced the buzz of talk among the groups of men he passed.

Near the front of the building an arrow with the one word 'Office' pointed towards a narrow metal stairway. He climbed to the upper floor, walked along another short length of corridor where the clatter of typewriters came from behind some of the frosted glass doors, then stopped at another door marked 'Mr W. Carter — Private.'

He tapped once, lightly, then opened the door and looked in. The man standing at a large desk near the window was too engrossed in the thin file of papers in his hands to realise he was being watched. But he jerked round in startled, momentarily angry surprise as Thane entered and let the door bang shut.

'What the — '

'Chief Inspector Thane, Millside C.I.D.,' Thane introduced himself briskly. 'Mr Hayston?'

'Oh.' The man swallowed, dropped the file back into one of the desk drawers, and closed the drawer with clumsy, embarrassed haste. 'Yes, I'm Hayston.'

'Good.' He glanced around. Carter's office had the carpeted floor and small cocktail cabinet which were the usual and necessary status symbols of any managing director. His sporting past was underlined by a miniature gallery of framed photographs lining the

12

walls — Carter in action in running vest and shorts, Carter in a track suit, Carter receiving an endless variety of cups and trophies with a broad smile on that thin, prominently-nosed face.

For the rest, the desk was big and glass-topped, there were a few filing cabinets along one wall, a heavy, modern safe, and the broad window looked out to the north-east, towards the centre of Glasgow.

'Well, ah . . . won't you sit down?' Peter Hayston dragged a chair forward and placed it near the desk. 'Cigarette?' He opened a small silver box on the desk, frowned, closed it again, and produced a leather case from his pocket.

'Thanks.' Thane took one of the cigarettes, found his own lighter while Hayston was still fumbling, then settled in the chair. He waited while the other man first hesitated then finally took the vacant seat behind the desk.

Peter Hayston hardly measured up to the conventional notion of a works manager. He was unusually small, probably just over five feet. He was young, Thane guessed still in his late twenties. A pinched, almost rabbit-like face was topped by a mop of thick dark hair, and he peered anxiously through a pair of heavy-framed spectacles. He wore a bright blue shirt and a red bow tie under a bronze-brown corduroy suit, the outfit completed by thickly soled suede shoes.

'It's all very dreadful.' Hayston blinked towards him and moistened his lips. 'This happening to Mr Carter . . . none of us can begin to believe it.'

'Any reason you know why he'd decide to come here over the weekend?'

'No.' Hayston took a deep breath. 'I can't think what happened.'

'But somebody shoved him in the enamelling oven,' said Thane bluntly. 'You know that, don't you?'

The eyes blinked faster and the mouth quivered. 'Yes — one of our men was with your sergeant when he found that note. And I can't think of any other way it could happen. That door can only be closed from the outside.'

Thane nodded. 'He wrote 'D help L'. His wife Lynne and — '

'I'd say David Stanley, his partner.'

'Where do we find him?'

Hayston shook his head. 'He's in Switzerland, carrying out some assessment tests on equipment. I've already cabled him — he's using an hotel near Lucerne as his base.'

Thane raised an eyebrow. 'Assessment tests for naval equipment — in Switzerland?'

14

'Marine application is only one aspect of hydrostatic work.' Hayston gave an impatient sigh. 'I'd give a lot to see him right now. And Mrs Carter out of town — '

'Leaves you running the show,' Thane finished it for him. 'My sergeant said you were running a check that nothing was missing. Everything intact?'

'Everything.' The works manager flushed. 'We take adequate precautions. All plans and drawings relating to classified work are gathered in at the end of each day.' He gestured towards the safe. 'They're kept in there. Everything taken out is signed for, and there's just as tight a system for returning.'

'How many staff on the payroll?'

'Including office personnel, a total of sixty-two.'

'But no watchman.'

'No.'

Thane raised an eyebrow. 'Yet you're doing work with a security classification.'

Hayston's rabbit chin firmed. 'There's a full system of burglar alarms. Mr Stanley personally supervised the installation.'

'Yet somebody got in — and out again. Carter's keys are missing. You've a set?'

'Yes.' The man fidgeted uneasily. 'So has Mr Stanley, and our head foreman.'

'Including a key to Carter's desk?' Thane

took a long draw on his cigarette and sat back, waiting.

Hayston showed a first flash of hostility. 'No, but the desk was unlocked when I came in. I thought — '

'Yes?'

'Well, that there might have been a note of where his wife is staying. All I know is she's in some London hotel.'

'What about the safe?'

'The two partners and myself know the combination.' The man's hands gripped the desk-top nervously. 'Look, Chief Inspector, nobody could have opened that safe before eight this morning. There's a time device fitted as well as the combination lock. I saw it set before I left here on Friday. I — wait a minute.' He reached out and stabbed a bell-push with one shaking finger. 'Ask his secretary, Jane Maulden. She was there.'

'Would she know the combination?'

'Well — yes, unofficially. Mrs Carter usually knows it, too. But no one else — I can guarantee it.'

A moment passed, then there was a light double-knock on the door. Thane turned and rose as it opened.

Jane Maulden was a raven-haired girl in her early twenties, good-looking in an open-air, high-breasted way. Her light make-up couldn't disguise the fact that she'd been crying, and the dark grey cloth of her high-necked slim-waisted dress served to accentuate the pallor of her face.

'Jane, this is the detective in charge of — of the investigations.' Hayston stumbled his way through the introductions.

'You can maybe help us on a couple of points,' said Thane, inwardly awarding the dead man full marks for his choice of secretary — on appearance, at any rate.

She nodded with a tight control. 'If I can.'

'It's about the safe — ' began Hayston.

Thane cut him short. 'Were you in this room on Friday when the safe was closed, Miss Maulden?'

'I had to be.' Her voice stayed low. 'One of my jobs is to check all classified plans and drawings have been returned.'

'And they were?' Thane saw her nod, and went on, 'Who else was here on Friday?'

'Mr Carter and — and Mr Hayston. Mr Carter set the time-lock.'

'For what time?'

'Monday at 8 a.m. — he asked me to check the setting before he closed the safe door.' She gave a not completely successful attempt at a smile. 'He usually did. He was worried he might choose the wrong day or something, then the whole plant would have been pretty

17

well at a standstill.'

'Just as I told you.' Hayston shot a quick, triumphant look towards Thane.

Thane ignored it. 'Has — did he ever come to the plant at the weekend?'

'Not often.' She bit lightly on her lower lip. 'Only when there was an important job on hand. But he certainly didn't mention it to me before this weekend.'

'Did he seem worried about anything?'

'No.' The tight control wavered for a moment. 'Even if he had been, he wouldn't have shown it. He — that wasn't his way.'

He thanked her, waited until she'd gone out and the door had closed, then walked over to the window. Hydrostat Drives' factory was on the outer edge of the Millside Division area, and he could see the last of the morning rush-hour traffic still speeding citywards along the new Glasgow Outer throughway. Further in, past the neat bungalows and high council house blocks, the dark bulk of the city was partly obscured by a gathering smoke haze. That meant there was little wind, and with only a few clouds in the sky the weather might hold fair.

He turned, to find Hayston watching him.

'Next on the list, this enamelling oven. What's it got to do with your normal production?'

18

Hayston shrugged. 'That was Mr Carter's idea. We were having to pay plenty to outside contractors for stove enamelling work on equipment casings. He decided we could do it ourselves and take in work from other firms when there was spare capacity.'

'It's an expensive plant?'

'Close on ten thousand pounds worth. But it's more than paying its way.'

Thane strode back towards the desk. 'How much training would it require to set that oven going?'

'Very little.' Hayston blinked his dislike of the question. 'There's a master control panel. For the stoving process, all that's required is to set a dial and press a couple of switches. The plant runs itself from there on.'

'No safety or warning devices inside the chamber?'

'Not as supplied.' The works manager hesitated then went on. 'We'd been thinking of fitting one, just this last week or so. A man was shut in by accident and wasn't missed for a few minutes. But he was all right — the heat was still at a low enough level.'

It fitted. A minor accident with no real consequence could have been enough to give someone an idea for the future.

'One other thing. Did Carter have a car?'

Hayston nodded. 'A blue Ford Executive. But he didn't use it very often. He usually took a bus part-way, then walked the rest — he liked the exercise.'

For a one-time athlete, the short walk was probably better than nothing. Thane stubbed his cigarette on the desk ashtray. 'That's it for now, Mr Hayston. Better give me the name of that hotel in Lucerne and a note of Carter's home address.'

The works manager reached for the pad in front of him, then stopped as Thane gripped him gently by the arm.

'Let's leave things as they are in here, Mr Hayston. I want this room locked — then I'll take the key. You'll get it back once the fingerprint team have finished.'

'But — ' Hayston blinked. 'If I'm to keep the plant running normally — '

'Your boss is lying dead in that damned oven downstairs,' snapped Thane. 'There'll be a man on guard outside this door and nobody gets in. That includes you, Mr Hayston. Understood?'

Behind the spectacle lenses, the small eyes seemed to fill with an angry moisture. But Hayston nodded.

★ ★ ★

The 10 a.m. coffee boil-up was going its rounds inside Millside station by the time the C.I.D. duty car deposited Colin Thane at the main entrance.

He stood on the pavement for a moment as the Jaguar purred off towards the parking area at the rear of the building. A cluster of children were playing on the opposite side of the road, kids from the tall, soot-grey tenements round about. Most of them looked in need of a bath, but he chuckled at the fierce intensity they concentrated on their game. One looked over, saw him, and stuck out his tongue. Thane winked, but took the hint and moved on.

Inside the building, the duty sergeant at the main uniformed bar counter was dealing with a couple of flustered, elderly women. In the background, a telephone bell was demanding an answer and the regional net radio was crackling a service message about a stolen car.

It was quieter upstairs, in the C.I.D. section. He walked through the main duty room with a nod to its solitary occupant, a detective constable typing a report, and shoved open the door of his own small office.

'Aye, I thought you were about due. That one's yours.' The small, lean figure sprawled in a chair in the middle of the room thumbed

21

towards the steaming mug of coffee balanced on the windowsill then took a cautious, unhappy sip at his own brew. Detective Inspector Moss had his own ideas about decent coffee, and they clashed head-on with those of the Millside canteen.

'Thanks, Phil.' Thane tossed his hat on the peg by the door, crossed over, and sank into the big, worn leather chair behind his desk with a sigh of relief. 'Well?'

Moss shrugged. 'You first. How's it shaping?'

'Rough.' Thane swung his feet up on the desk, took out his cigarettes, and lit one. He caught Moss's lifted eyebrow and shoved pack and lighter towards him. 'Here.'

'Graciously given.' Moss helped himself, his face still gloomy. 'What's happening?'

'Carter's wife is on holiday but nobody knows where, his partner is adrift somewhere in Switzerland, and if the note he left is any guide he didn't know who killed him or why.'

'Some start,' agreed Moss sardonically.

Thane was the younger man, just nudging into his early forties. Phil Moss admitted to being in his mid-fifties, but never got down to details — and age was only the start of the difference between them.

Dark-haired, with a cheerfully rugged face, Colin Thane was married, with a wife, two school-age children, and a bungalow home in the suburbs. He carried his powerful, slightly overweight build with a fluid ease left over from his days as a beat cop when he'd twice been in the Police Boxing Federation heavyweight finals — and twice, he had to admit, had promptly been beaten close to a pulp.

Phil Moss, on the other hand, was a bachelor by grim determination. A small, grey man with sparse, sandy hair, he looked more like an overworked office clerk than a policeman — except that office clerks don't last long if they wear baggy, unpressed suits, crumpled shirt collars, and have a general down-at-heel air. Moss didn't care. His main devotion in life, the barometer of his outlook, was the state of the stomach ulcer which he guarded with a massive collection of remedies against the threat of a surgeon's knife.

That ulcer and its treatments was famed throughout the city's divisional offices.

But the chuckles still held respect. Thane and Moss formed a highly efficient team — and an underlying friendship was only part of the secret.

'Hydrostat Drives are on the security list.' Thane gathered his coffee from the window-sill and took a long, happy swallow. 'We'll have the cloak-and-dagger outfits asking questions before long.'

'They've already started.' Moss flicked a slip of paper towards him. 'Office of the C. in C. North Atlantic, Clyde area — a Commander Allowes of Admiralty security. That's his number and will you call him?' He grunted. 'Talks through his teeth and sounds unhappy.'

'What about Headquarters?' Thane propped the reminder against his telephone.

'They want a progress report by noon — and they're moaning about not getting last week's crime returns.' The latter annoyed Moss. 'I left the thing on your desk on Friday, ready for signing.'

'It's around.' Thane dragged open the top drawer of his desk, found the return sheet among a bundle of papers, located a pen, and scribbled his signature on the space marked 'Divisional Officer.'

'Good.' Moss took it from him. 'Now, what about Carter?'

'Once I've organised a few things we go out to his house. There just might have been a visitor — his keys are missing.' He ticked off the rest. 'MacMaster and Doc Williams will do the p.m., I'm checking with the Scientific Bureau in another hour, and I've left MacLeod interviewing his way round the plant. He's got three men with him, enough to eat the job.'

Moss nodded. 'If it helps, the uniformed branch are contacting all beat men in the area — one of them might have noticed something out of the ordinary.'

Thane rubbed one thumb along his chin. 'Phil, do a couple of things for me. See if Records have anything on a Peter Hayston, age a little under thirty, slight build, wears glasses. He's works manager and maybe not quite so soft round the edges as he makes out. Then ask Motor Taxation to dig up the licence number of a blue Ford Executive — Carter's car. I've an idea we're going to be looking for it soon.'

'How about wife and partner?'

'I'll take care of them.' He thought for a moment. 'When you've a chance, I want a breakdown of the company's financial background.'

'Right.' Moss rose to go.

'Phil . . . ' Thane leaned forward, a more personal note in his voice. 'What happened this morning? Did you find him?'

Moss's mouth tightened. 'Yes, and ended up being told to mind my own damned business.'

After five years residence in her boarding house, Phil Moss had to confess a reluctant affection for his landlady, Emma Robertson.

And he'd sensed something wrong the moment the widow had returned home from a two-week seaside holiday full of a fluttering femininity which, by Moss's standards, was all wrong for a woman turned fifty — even a well-preserved example of her undoubted calibre.

She'd dropped her bombshell on the Saturday — she was going to remarry, and her husband-to-be was coming round on Sunday evening.

Which was bad enough, considering Emma Robertson's previous coddling care of Moss's wildly varying ulcer diets and the way she darned his socks, sewed buttons on his shirts, and generally fought to keep him what she described as 'halfway decent looking.'

But when he saw Arthur Robert 'Splits' Clark, six months out of Perth Prison after doing a five-year stretch, march up to the boarding house and disappear into Emma Robertson's parlour things became serious.

'He's living in a commercial hotel out near Queen's Park,' growled Moss. 'I got him there at breakfast this morning. He sat there and told me he'd been expecting me round.'

'What's his story?'

'That he's got a job as an engraver, that he's going straight, that if I try to foul things up between him and 'his Emma' he'll sue me

26

for damages.' Moss felt a familiar grumbling begin to gather in his stomach, a sure warning of too intense an involvement. 'His story is that there's a 'bond of warm affection' between them. Aye, I'll bet — the house alone's worth a few thousand.'

'I thought Splits Clark had a wife,' mused Thane.

'The divorce decree becomes absolute next month. He says Emma Robertson knows all about it.'

'But not about Splits Clark.' Thane had to admit that was far from pleasant.

Arthur Robert Clark's nickname came from an ability to split the thin paper of a pound note along its length with a razor blade and make two notes from one. But his real trade was the counterfeit game, and his last conviction had been for mass-producing dollar-value travellers' cheques.

'What do I do now?' appealed Moss. 'Tell her?'

'You can't and you'd better not try,' warned Thane quickly. 'Clark's on solid ground — if you tell Emma Robertson about his record any lawyer could take you to the cleaners.' He suppressed a grin with an effort. 'None of this would have happened if you'd asked her the same question, as you should have, years back.'

'Thanks.' Moss threw him a glare and went out, slamming the door in indignant protest.

Thane chuckled, swallowed the last of the coffee, then got to work. A few minutes later, when a young police cadet orderly answered his buzzer's summons, he had two messages ready for the communications room. The first was to the Interpol clearing office at Geneva, asking the Swiss police to advise David Stanley of his partner's death and then to make a check on where he'd been for the last few days. The second, equally terse, was to the London Metropolitan force, asking them to locate the hotel where Lynne Carter was staying, break the news, and make equally sure of where she'd been since she left home.

'That's all for now, son.' As the cadet went out, he reached for the telephone. The switchboard was slow to answer, and he rapped the receiver rest impatiently.

'Yes, sir?' The girl operator's voice held a touch of ice as she came on the line.

He gave the Admiralty office number then, when he was connected, asked for Commander Allowes. A buzz and a click, and he heard a receiver lift.

'Allowes here.' The voice was clipped and precise.

'Thane, Millside C.I.D. You called me earlier.'

'The Hydrostat Drives business.' The sailor made it sound like the title of some obscene book. 'You know they're on the special list?'

'I'm keeping it in mind,' said Thane neutrally. 'Up till now there's no sign of a security aspect.'

He heard a sniff. Allowes, whatever his background, seemed to have little confidence in workaday policemen. 'I'd advise very careful consideration of the possibility, Chief Inspector. It's early for us to be officially involved, but . . . '

'But let's keep any secrets we've still got left, eh?' Thane didn't bother to cloak the sarcasm behind his words. 'How important is the Hydrostat contract work?'

'Too important to discuss over a telephone.' The voice chilled several degrees.

'How about in terms of money value?'

He heard a sigh of annoyance. 'Does that have any bearing?'

'Probably a damned sight more than your usual ideas of little men in false beards running around stealing plans,' said Thane heavily. 'But if you feel that way about things I'll put it through official channels — from the top down.'

'Well . . . ' Allowes digested the implied threat. 'The initial contract, fifty thousand. Future contract work, perhaps half a million pounds — but spread over several years.'

Thane whistled. 'That's a lot of money!'

'We pay sophisticated prices for sophisticated gear,' said the Admiralty man with an unexpected touch of humour. 'I think — yes, I think maybe I'd better come and see you. This afternoon?'

'Fine.' Another thought struck Thane. 'Isn't there always a full security check on all employees when a firm goes on the special list?'

'We call it routine background evaluation,' corrected Allowes. 'Why?'

'I'd like to see the Hydrostat results.'

'Hmm. Perhaps.' A click came from the other end, and the line went dead.

Thane swore to himself and slowly replaced the receiver. He sat very still for a moment, then lit another cigarette. As he took his first draw of the smoke, the telephone rang — long and angrily.

He scooped it up. 'Thane.'

'Sergeant MacLeod, sir — '

'Still at the factory?' Thane felt a sudden surge of interest.

'Yes, sir. Nothing fresh here. But if you want Mrs Carter, she's just been on the telephone. I spoke to her myself.'

'Eh?' Thane coughed on his cigarette smoke. 'Where is she?'

'At home.' Sergeant MacLeod liked saving his surprises till the end. 'According to her, Carter 'phoned her on Saturday and said it was vital she was back here today. That's all I know, but — '

Thane cut him short. 'We'll handle it from here, Mac — and thanks.' He put down the receiver, tapped his fingers briefly on the desk, then lifted the 'phone again.

This time the switchboard answered quickly.

'Sir?'

'Tell Inspector Moss to meet me at the front door — and get the duty car round.'

He hung up, and for the first time noticed the brand new manilla folder Moss had placed to one side of his desk.

It was headed 'Murder of William Carter.'

It was still empty.

Well, maybe they'd have something for it soon.

2

The blue-uniformed driver whistled half-heartedly to himself as he edged the C.I.D. duty car through the busy mid-morning traffic, along streets where parking space was at a premium and pedestrians huddled like sheep waiting for a chance to cross. A heavy truck swung across his front without signalling and he cursed mildly then picked up the tune again without missing a note.

Behind him, Colin Thane sat quietly, watching the familiar scene through half-shut eyes while Phil Moss sucked impassively on a bismuth tablet and listened to the busy chatter coming from the radio.

A couple of Southern Division cars had their hands full rounding up a bunch of neds who'd booted in a jeweller's window near Eglinton Street. Headquarters Control, asking for any car free in the Eastern Division to handle a road accident, was having no takers. Somewhere in Central Division a C.I.D. observation van was being recalled from watch on a bookie's office — the customer wanted had been picked up by another mobile.

Routine stuff . . . it made up most of the day in Glasgow's seven police divisions, responsible between them for a population of considerably more than a million. Leave aside the parking tickets, the drunks, the minor brawls and petty annoyances, and it came down to a regular one hundred crimes a day, every day.

Moss gave a gentle belch. 'There's one consolation, Colin. The Carter woman knows he's dead by now, and that's one job I don't mind avoiding.'

Thane kept his eye on the traffic but nodded. 'It helps. How did you make out on the company background?'

'In half an hour?' His second-in-command crunched the bismuth in sheer indignation. 'Give me a chance!'

Thane gave an apologetic shrug. When it came to a burrowing research job Phil Moss was best left alone to set his own pace. Totalling up figures or drafting reports, analysing the Trend of Crime graphs or tooth-combing his way through some minor mountain of documentation, Moss was in his element . . . though his thin, wiry frame could be equally to the fore when things reached the blood and batons stage.

Sometimes, Thane envied him — and had few illusions about his own less patient outlook. He knew the rules, he disciplined himself to follow them most of the time, he'd take scientific aid from anyone down to a Congo witch-doctor if it looked like helping. But every now and again he'd throw the lot overboard, strike out on a hunch — then be prepared to sweat out the result.

That was when Moss most often came to the rescue. By not having a chip on his shoulder because a younger man outranked him. By possessing a gift of stony-faced insolence. And particularly through usually conjuring up a way which gave the Millside chief a second chance if things went wrong.

For once, Headquarters had done something sensible when they'd teamed them together in an unlikely partnership, Thane straight from a roving commission on the regional crime squad, Moss tired of life as a Headquarters special duty officer.

And Millside Division had never been quite the same since.

Thane chuckled at the thought, and drew a suspicious glare.

'Nothing,' he assured his companion.

Moss grunted, and unwrapped another bismuth tablet as the car swung on to the West throughway, its speed increasing. His ulcer was acting up. Sometimes the cause was the sheer tension of a case, but this time —

A decent woman like Emma Robertson and a smooth-faced character like Splits Clark.

Ach, it didn't bear thinking.

★   ★   ★

William Carter's home was a large, new ranch-style bungalow in Monkswalk, one of the few plush, residential sections in Millside Division . . . part of it, in fact, was Northern Division territory, but the whole was treated as common ground by the two stations.

The duty car cruised slowly down one broad, shrub-lined avenue, their driver located the number he wanted, and they swung in through wide entrance gates, along a broad sweep of concrete driveway fringed with close-mown lawns, then stopped near the house door.

'Nice place.' Thane glanced around, then thumbed towards the other car already parked ahead. 'That's nice, too.'

'Aye.' It was a low-slung, smooth-lined Alfa coupé, finished in an unobtrusive black, travel-stained, but holding a promise of power in every line. Moss sniffed. 'Expense account motoring. Somebody just took a quick peek at us from the house, Colin.'

'I saw.'

They left the driver on radio watch and got out. Thane led the way up the short flight of steps to the front door, pressed the bell, and waited. A moment or two passed, and then it opened.

'Good morning.' She was tall and fair, not more than thirty, with a professional model's figure and carriage. She wore dark blue tailored slacks with a crisply laundered shirt-blouse in a light grey cotton silk. A dark blue ribbon held the cascade of natural blonde hair back from her forehead and her feet were snug in soft leather moccasins.

'Mrs Carter?'

She nodded. Lynne Carter was a good-looking woman, self-assured, and Thane could see no particularly red-eyed signs of grief. The bronzed tan of her skin, going down into the deep V of that shirt-blouse, hadn't been obtained on any local holiday beach. Her careful make-up must have taken time, and though her expression held a nervous strain she was not quite the standard example of a woman who'd only just found herself to be a widow.

'Millside C.I.D. Chief Inspector Thane and' — he beckoned Moss forward — 'Detective Inspector Moss.'

'Come in, please.' The voice held a slight huskiness. 'I'm sorry the place is in — well, rather a mess. But I wasn't expected back. The housekeeper's off on a long weekend.'

They went in and she closed the door.

'I'm sorry about this, Mrs Carter,' said Thane, laying his hat on the hallway table and nudging Moss to do the same.

She gave a faint, almost weary shrug. 'Hearing it had happened was the biggest shock. But I'm all right now.'

They followed her into the big front room, a place where lime green fitted carpets and a slightly lighter shade of velvet curtains contrasted with pure white walls and set a whole tone of expensively simple taste. But Thane's immediate interest was the man standing by the big stone-framed fireplace. He was tall, bulky, with thick dark hair and a beard to match, framing a broad, sleepy-eyed face — sleepy-eyed yet still obviously alert. One large hand rested on the fireplace, the other was deep in a pocket of the maroon anorak he wore over sports slacks and a roll-necked jersey.

'My husband's partner, David Stanley,' introduced the blonde.

'Eh?' Phil Moss showed his surprise.

'Something wrong?' Stanley looked from one detective to the other.

'You're supposed to be in Switzerland,' said Moss.

'That?' Stanley scuffed his feet on the thick carpeting. 'I was. But I flew back yesterday after Bill telephoned me.'

'He called you, too?' Thane raised an eyebrow. 'We didn't know.'

The bearded face grimaced. 'Well, it doesn't matter much now. He spoke to me late on Saturday night, I flew into London yesterday, collected Lynne at her hotel and we drove up together overnight. We only got here about an hour ago.' He paused and pursed his lips. 'Maybe I'd better let Lynne finish the introductions.'

She did. David Stanley had a handclasp in line with his appearance, strong and slow, yet somehow alert.

'Right.' He turned to his dead partner's wife, a softer note in his voice. 'Lynne, maybe you should sit down for a spell.' He nodded approvingly as she obeyed. 'Well now — just what's happened, Chief Inspector? All Lynne got when she spoke to the plant was the start of a garbled story from our works manager, then some policeman on the line.'

'Detective Sergeant MacLeod,' confirmed Thane. 'He was the first officer to go to the plant.'

Stanley brushed that aside. 'Anyway, between them she was told Bill was dead and that it wasn't just an accident. She was to stay right here and somebody would come out.' His eyes narrowed a little. 'If it wasn't an accident then — well, what did happen?'

Phil Moss had walked over to the window but was watching. So was Lynne Carter from her chair, her lips a tight, expectant line.

'It looks like murder,' said Thane quietly. 'I'm sorry, Mrs Carter.'

David Stanley took a deep breath. 'How did he die?'

'It wasn't very pleasant.' Thane paused and glanced towards the woman.

'Go on.' White teeth showed briefly as she bit her lower lip. 'I want to know.'

'As far as we can make out it happened some time yesterday. He was locked inside the enamelling room and somebody — well, somebody switched on the machinery.'

'Oh, hell . . . ' Stanley groaned aloud. 'Then the heat — '

'Was set for 250 degrees,' contributed Moss grimly. 'We can't say how long he lasted.'

Lynne Carter made a sudden choking noise. She rose quickly to her feet and almost ran from the room, the door banging shut behind her.

Stanley started for the door, then hesitated. 'Should I — '

Thane shook his head. 'Leave her. It's usually better.'

'Right.' The man seemed relieved. He fumbled in his anorak pockets, found his cigarettes, lit one, and took a long draw. 'Could you use a drink?'

'Not for us,' declared Thane. 'But go ahead.'

'I will.' He crossed the room, opened the door of a small, glass-fronted cupboard and produced the nearest bottle and a glass. A stiff measure of whisky gurgled out. He put the bottle down, picked up the glass, and drank most of it at a gulp. 'This kind of thing is raw on the nerves, and I only had a couple of hours sleep on the drive up.'

'That's your car outside?'

'No, it's Lynne's. But I did most of the motoring.' He sighed. 'Why kill Bill? Are you looking for some head-case character or — well, did he walk into a robbery?'

'We don't know yet.' Thane lowered himself into the nearest of the big armchairs. 'But we want to find out, and so do Admiralty security.'

Stanley stood where he was, frowning. 'That figures maybe more than you know, Chief Inspector.'

'Tell me about this telephone call,' invited Thane. 'What did Carter say to make you

40

come back so quickly?'

'That's what I mean.' Stanley finished the rest of the whisky and nursed the empty glass reflectively. 'He told me we had trouble on our hands, real trouble, and he wasn't sure what to do about it. I was to collect Lynne in London and we were to meet him here, at the house, this morning.'

'You still haven't said what kind of trouble.' Thane leaned forward, his voice crisping.

'Because I don't know,' confessed Stanley. 'Some of — no, most of our stuff's on Government classified listing. It might have been — well, I don't know. He said he couldn't talk on an open telephone line, but he sounded worried, worried sick. And Bill wasn't the kind to panic without plenty of reason.'

'You've no idea?'

'No. But right now it could be any of half a dozen things.'

Moss had been listening silently, a querulous expression growing on his thin face. He cleared his throat. 'Any financial problems, Mr Stanley? As a firm, I mean?'

The man gave a firm shake of his head. 'Look around you,' he invited. 'Bill Carter bought this place outright. I've a nice healthy balance in the bank, and the firm's books are well in the black.' He laid down his glass. 'Do

41

you know why I was in Switzerland?'

Thane rubbed a thumb along his chin. 'Hayston said you were testing equipment.'

'Equipment!' David Stanley chuckled, warming to his subject. 'Marine application is only one side of hydrostatic drive, Chief Inspector. We've been up to our necks developing road vehicle transmissions — no clutch, no gearbox, no drive shafts. Just small-bore pipes leading to each wheel — push a pedal with your toe and you go forward, push the same pedal with your heel and you reverse. All done by oil pressure, no nonsense about gear ratios, no need to ever touch a brake pedal. It makes everything else on the roads look like a hangover from the horse and buggy era.'

'Wait a minute.' Thane's brow wrinkled as he dredged his memory. 'Weren't there some demonstrations a year or two back?'

'The National Engineering Laboratory circus?' Stanley nodded. 'It was fairly primitive. We're away beyond that stage — and we have to be, because plenty of the big boys on both sides of the Atlantic are hard at work on this. We've installed our version in two vehicles, a private car and a three-ton truck, and I had the car over with me doing a final work-out on some of the Swiss passes. The next stage is a series of Ministry of

Defence tests up in the Highlands this coming week.'

'Important?'

'Very. If we're lucky, the contracts we could land for a.f.v. transmission — armoured fighting vehicles, tanks, scout cars, that sort of thing — could make our Admiralty work look like pin money.'

'Could you handle so much extra work?' queried Moss.

'No, but we could licence it — and Hydrostat Drives Incorporated has everything buttoned up in nice, tight design patents.'

Thane nodded, sensing the rest. The vast NATO market for armoured vehicles was only a start, leading to commercial transport, the everyday motor industry — provided the price was right, the benefits evident and that mass production techniques could cope, the firm's future could be rich and limitless.

'But you didn't bring the test car back with you?'

'No. There wasn't time. Anyway the operation was near enough to complete and we'd already made arrangements. I left the rest of our team to wrap things up on their own, and we've a plane chartered to fly them home with the car tomorrow.'

The door behind them clicked open. Thane glanced round, then rose from his chair as

Lynne Carter came in. Her face pale, her make-up no longer such a picturebook perfection, she walked across the room, took a cigarette from a gilt box on the mantelshelf, then used a matching lighter.

'Lynne?' David Stanley left the rest unsaid.

'Fine now.' She gave them a faint, reassuring smile. 'I'm sorry. It was — well, just a little too much for me.'

'That's understandable.' Thane eyed his wrist watch. 'We're just about finished for the moment, Mrs Carter. Except for a couple of questions I'd like you to answer.'

She nodded. 'Go ahead.'

'Did your husband tell you why it was so important you came back for this meeting?'

'No. He said exactly the same to me as he did to David — that the firm had trouble on its hands, and that we'd have to decide right away what we were going to do.'

'You'd been away for a few days?'

'Since last Tuesday morning — and before you ask, he was perfectly happy when I left. We even spoke by 'phone on Thursday night, and everything was fine as far as he was concerned.'

'Eh, Mrs Carter . . . ' Moss scratched himself absently behind one ear. 'Even if there was trouble at the factory what would it have to do with you? Did he always come asking your advice when a problem turned up?'

Stanley answered for her. 'She'd every right to expect to be asked, Inspector. I thought you'd know — we're a private limited company with only three directors, Bill Carter, Lynne and myself.'

Moss eyed him shrewdly. 'Equal share-holdings?'

'No, and I'll have to put a lawyer on the job before we can be sure what the position is now.' Stanley showed a gathering impatience. 'There's a lot that I'll need to start doing . . .'

'And we won't hold you back from it,' said Thane, accepting the man's mood. 'We'll need routine statements later, of course. You'll be here, Mrs Carter?'

She nodded.

'I'll be down at the factory,' Stanley told them. He frowned. 'What about — I mean, will you need anyone to identify the body?'

'That's taken care of already,' Thane assured him.

'Then I'll see you out.'

They went with him through the hallway to the front door. On the porch outside, Stanley raised a detaining hand.

'You've a job to do, Chief Inspector. But if you need information I can help on most things — and save Lynne being harried.'

'We'll try to remember,' said Thane briskly. 'Any idea where Carter's car is kept?'

'There's a garage round at the back. The car's inside, locked up. He often preferred — '

'To walk, I know.' Thane spent a moment admiring the broad, immaculately kept garden. 'That makes it more of a problem to build up an idea of his movements. And with the housekeeper away, he'd be alone here. Can you think of any friend who might have dropped in on a visit?'

David Stanley stuck his hands deep in the anorak's pockets, his brow puckering. 'None off hand, unless one of the neighbours looked in. Most of what he called his 'free time' he was liable to spend on paperwork brought home from the plant.'

'We'll check around.'

The burly bearded figure watched from the porch until they'd climbed back aboard the duty car.

'Well?' queried Moss as the car started up. 'Where now?'

'Headquarters.' Thane lounged back against the leather upholstery as they began moving. Stanley had gone back inside and the house door was closed. 'Scientific Branch first.'

'I hate to say it,' mused Moss unhappily. 'But this 'trouble' Carter talked about could be he'd found somebody nobbling factory blueprints.'

'Admiralty stuff, or details about this new car transmission?' Thane wound down the passenger window and let some fresh air stir around the car's interior as they travelled along. 'Nothing's impossible. But I'd like to know more about this Carter and Stanley partnership, and how Lynne Carter fitted into the situation.'

'Aye.' Moss nodded a sardonic understanding. 'It's a pretty ill wind which doesn't blow somebody a good turn. Still, I'd say their story should be easy enough to check.'

'I'm glad,' said Thane blandly. 'That's just what you're going to do this afternoon, Phil. You can start once we've had something to eat.'

'To eat?' Moss stirred hopefully. 'Where?'

'The canteen at Headquarters.'

'On a Monday?' Moss thought of what that usually meant, and suppressed a groan.

★ ★ ★

Some time in the future there was a plan and a promise for a new Headquarters building. But for the time being the squat, soot-stained block in St Andrews Street still fulfilled its role. Close to the city mortuary, the High Court building, the river Clyde and a working men's hostel, a stone's throw from the gaunt struggling parkland of Glasgow Green on one side and the bustling traffic of the Salt-market on the other, it was a crowded, busy hive where office space was at a premium.

It was close on noon when the Millside duty car deposited its two C.I.D. passengers at the main door. Inside Headquarters, with its white-tiled corridors and vaguely antiseptic odour, they parted company — Moss bound for the tranquil files of the Records Office, Thane heading up towards the Scientific Bureau's top floor territory.

He arrived there as a group of men, some twenty in number, came pouring out, feet clattering on the stone floor of the corridor, their voices mingling in a confusion of accents and languages.

Once they'd passed, he went in. Superintendent Laurence, the Bureau head, a fat, untidy man with a shock of unruly white hair, an inevitable dribble of old cigarette ash down his waistcoat and his hands deep in his pockets, was standing beside one of the laboratory benches.

He saw Thane and came over. 'Been expecting you, Colin.'

Thane thumbed towards the doorway. 'Giving guided tours now, Dan?'

'Aye.' Laurence gave a heavy sniff. 'They're an overseas police study group on methods — ballistics mainly. The Chief Constable volunteered us for it at the last Interpol conference . . . great man for volunteerin' you first then tellin' you later. And they're bright enough boys — with a ruddy pocketful o' questions to keep us on the hop.' He led the way into his office, swept a bundle of papers off the only spare chair and jerked his head towards it. 'Rest your feet, man. I'll see what's ready for you.'

'Thanks.' Thane swung the chair round and draped himself over it, saddle-fashion. 'I need anything you've got.'

'What's unusual about that?' The Bureau chief grinned, swung back towards the doorway, and gave a shout. 'Tommy — '

'Sir?' The reply floated back from somewhere outside.

'That Millside job, and hurry up.' Laurence turned back to his visitor, gruffly apologetic. 'I'd have gone out on it myself, but it's just been one of those mornings. Still, the lads I sent out know their business, none better.' He broke off as a young detective constable in a white laboratory coat knocked briefly on the opened door.

49

'Carter murder, sir.' The D.C. laid a thin file on the desk. 'All we've got through so far, at any rate.' He eyed the bureau chief carefully. 'I'm not completely happy about the time lock on their safe, sir. Mind if I go back and take another look at it this afternoon?'

'We'll do better than that,' decided Laurence. 'I'll come with you, an' keep your mind off wee diversions like chatting up the office girls.'

'Right, sir.' The D.C. grinned and went out.

'Now then, let's see what we've got.' Laurence squeezed behind his desk, sat down, and began thumbing through the report sheets. 'Aye, here's one bit that interests me. When do you expect the p.m. report, Colin?'

'Some time this evening.'

'Uh-huh. Then when you do, Carter's blood group should be interesting. The lads found some small blood-stains — droplets, not much more — on his clothing and on the floor near that enamelling control panel. Somebody got punched on the nose.'

Thane raised an eyebrow. 'Stretching it out a little, aren't you?'

'In this department nothing is stretched — except maybe my temper.' Laurence took out an oilskin pouch, hand-rolled himself a cigarette from the makings it contained, and lit the resultant cylinder with a brief flaring of loose tobacco. 'The blood is Group B and microscopic examination shows traces of nasal mucus.' He busied himself on the report again, one nicotine-stained forefinger running its way down the typewritten wordage. 'We date the blood-stains at less than forty-eight hours old, if it helps. Nothing much on fingerprints, though.'

'That's no surprise.' Fingerprint techniques kept advancing, like the new soft X-ray and lead dust routine pioneered by Laurence's department and a team of Glasgow radiologists, a technique which could find prints on human skin and many another surface previously regarded as impossible. But these days anyone who left fingerprints behind was either careless or downright stupid.

'Still — ' Laurence read on silently for a few seconds. 'The control panel had been wiped, and the same with the door handle to the enamelling chamber. The only fresh prints belonged to the foreman who found the body. There were plenty of prints in Carter's office, and we're still working on them.' He took time for a long draw on his cigarette. 'There's no sign of interference with locks or windows anywhere in the plant, Colin, except at Carter's desk. A key had been jammed in the lock of one drawer — it opened, but the key's tip broke off inside the lock. That's all we've got for now.'

Thane sighed a little and leaned forward in his chair. The Scientific Bureau's facts might well hold their own importance, but for the moment they were just a loose scattering of bits and pieces in an otherwise unknown emptiness.

'Dan, it might pay to give Carter's home the once-over. And there's a car in his garage.'

'We'll take care of that,' promised Laurence. 'Eh . . . you know there's an Admiralty interest in all this?'

'It's been mentioned,' agreed Thane. 'Much more of it, and I'll feel there's a little man in a sailor suit perched on my shoulder. Why?'

Laurence shrugged. 'I've been told to send them a copy of any Bureau findings. I thought you'd like to know.' The telephone by his elbow gave a shrill ring. He lifted it, answered with a grunt, listened, made a silent grimace, then grunted again. 'He's here. I'll tell him. 'Bye.' The receiver was replaced with finger-and-thumb disgust. 'The acting temporary kingpin, Colin — he wants to see you.'

Thane sighed. Chief Superintendent William 'Buddha' Ilford, head of the city's C.I.D., was on autumn leave. His deputy, Superintendent Donfoot, hardly topped the popularity poll.

'I'll get it over with.' He rose to his feet. 'Dan, you don't happen to have a recipe handy that guarantees a nice, even temper?'

'Me?' Laurence chuckled. 'If I had, it would have made my fortune in this place a long time ago.'

* * *

It took a full twenty minutes before Colin Thane managed to escape from Superintendent Donfoot's grasp. The acting C.I.D. chief, a thin, toothy vulture of a man with a distant university background, maintained a desk where every last pencil was arranged with military precision — and believed that everything in life was a matter of organised effort. But his most annoying trait was the way he punctuated every other sentence with a brisk snap of his fingers. Intended to show the ease and simplicity of what he suggested, it was more inclined to encourage his subordinates to thoughts of instant mayhem.

The interview itself didn't matter. It boiled down to the fact that Superintendent Donfoot, one week of his reign remaining, would be most upset if the Carter case wasn't wrapped up in a neat package labelled 'solved' before Buddha Ilford returned.

'Admiralty interest, newspaper interest, the whole thing amounts to an opportunity, Thane.' The fingers snapped once more. 'Now's your chance to show that the civil arm isn't sleeping on what could be a possible security matter.'

'Yes, sir.' Thane stood wooden-faced, trying to tune out the voice, the fingersnaps, the face, everything about Donfoot's presence.

'Progress doesn't amount to much so far.' Donfoot frowned his displeasure. 'Still, as long as you ensure a properly organised approach, the results will come. Ah — you've seen the mid-day editions?'

Thane shook his head.

'Here we are, then.' Donfoot had the two evening papers ready in the middle tray of his desk. He spread them out, waiting for comment.

Both papers had made the story front-page news, though somewhat overshadowed by the latest political ruckus in Whitehall. Thane glanced over the stories, in each case supported by stock photographs of Carter in running kit.

'I gave a press conference, of course,' said Donfoot chattily. 'Doesn't do to tell these fellows too much, but saying too little can create just as difficult a situation.'

Thane grunted politely. If Donfoot liked some personal publicity that was his business. The news desks had a murder story and were happy — even if the automatic restriction of Government 'D' notices meant they could only describe Hydrostat Drives as 'a city engineering firm.' 'D' stood for Defence of the Realm, and editors who broke a D notice were in the worst kind of trouble, trouble right up to their necks.

Donfoot leaned forward and tapped one paragraph with his forefinger. 'This is the attitude we'll maintain for the moment, Thane — 'police are engaged in following up a firm line of investigation.'' His voice oozed equal portions of encouragement and warning. 'A firm line, Thane. With an early development.'

When he escaped, Colin Thane made straight for the Headquarters canteen on the ground floor. In the inspectors' room, where there was waitress service, most of the tables were already busy. But Phil Moss had managed to save one over in a corner.

'You're late,' he accused, toying with the omelette in front of him. 'What happened?'

'A touch of Donfoot disease.' Thane slumped thankfully into his chair, read the menu, and gave his order for stew, apple pie and coffee to the hovering waitress. Moss added a glass of milk for himself, then chuckled.

'They've got it worked out in Central Division that he's due to retire in another three years, two months and five days — or is it four? Anyway, how about Dan Laurence?'

He listened to Thane's account, occasionally forking another mouthful of omelette. Then he gave his own news.

'Records have nothing on the works manager, but I thought I'd look up a few other names. Carter's partner is a surprise.'

'Stanley?' Thane broke off as the first part of his order arrived. He thanked the waitress, then leaned across the table. 'What about him?'

'Our big, bluff David Stanley seems to have a temper when roused — two convictions for assault, the last only eighteen months back.' Moss abandoned what was left of the omelette and sipped his milk. 'The first charge drew a fine, but last time it was sixty days without the option. He was in a brawl in a gambling club and broke somebody's jaw.'

'So he might get angry enough with his partner and — no, that's not it.' Thane shook his head. 'I'm not forgetting Dan Laurence's business about someone having their nose thumped. But the kind of man who'll press a

56

switch and leave his victim to die the hard way doesn't have a hot temper. He's the opposite, cold as ice.'

'I won't argue.' Moss watched his companion sample the stew. The sight made him vaguely envious, but stew was out as far as his ulcer was concerned — every diet sheet he'd collected agreed on that. 'Well, here's another little surprise. I managed to trace the firm's lawyer through the Company Registration lists — his name's Scheven, and he's more used to looking up textbooks than dealing with cops. But he came round eventually — Hydrostat Drives Incorporated has only three directors, just the way Stanley told us. The original partnership was signed four years back, giving a share split of sixty per cent to Carter and forty per cent to Stanley on a nominal £10,000 capital.'

'When did Lynne Carter come in then?'

'When Carter married her about two years ago. His wedding present was exactly one-quarter of his holdings.'

Slowly, Thane laid down his fork. 'A quarter!' He whistled softly. The tall, newly widowed blonde's overall shareholding might have only amounted to a minority fifteen per cent — but placed alongside her husband's remaining holdings or Stanley's forty per cent it gave her final control in any disagreement between the partners.

Moss wasn't finished. 'This lawyer Scheven had another wee thing to tell me. Carter's will leaves the lot to his wife.'

It was a motive all right, plain and old fashioned but by no means out of date. Thane finished his stew in silence, tackled the apple pie, then caught Moss looking at him in a strange, almost belligerent way.

'Don't tell me there's more?'

'No — at least, not about the Carter business.'

Thane read the signs. 'Your landlady? Now look, Phil — '

Moss didn't let him finish. 'Colin, how about coming round this evening, just for a spell? Splits Clark shouldn't be there and — well, maybe you can have a word with her.'

'Me?' Thane sighed. 'What good will that do?' But his second-in-command didn't often ask favours. 'All right, if there's time — but don't expect any miracles.'

Once they'd finished the meal and had left the canteen, he left Moss to locate their car and driver while he used the telephone callbox near the main door. The first call he made was to Millside Division. All was quiet, the C.I.D. desk assured him. Detective Sergeant MacLeod had 'phoned in from the Hydrostat factory, but purely to report that most of his work was finished. There was a slight and separate problem down in the dockland area, where a couple of neds had bungled an attempt to rob a seaman. One ned was in hospital and the other was still running.

He told the desk to circulate the second ned's description, hung up, lit a cigarette, then lifted the receiver again and asked for his home number.

The burr of the ringing tone came back along the line for a full thirty seconds before it was answered by a young, breathless voice.

'It's me, Tommy,' he told his son. 'Is your mum in?'

'Yes, but — '

'Get her, will you?'

He heard the receiver thumped down on the hall table and waited what seemed a long time before Mary's voice sounded over the wires.

'Colin?' There was the same slightly breathless note in her voice. 'Trust you to 'phone at the wrong moment.'

'What's going on?' he demanded, sensing the rueful humour in her voice. 'Another row with the milkman?'

'No. The car won't start, and I've got the kids helping to push.'

'Flat battery?' The car was elderly,

second-hand and inclined to be temperamental.

'Flatter than flat, but I'll have another try before I call the garage.'

'I'll be late home,' he told her. 'Among other things, Phil wants me to look in on his landlady.'

'Mrs Robertson?' Mary Thane was immediately interested. She'd heard the Splits Clark story over supper the previous night. 'She needs somebody to talk sense into her.' Her manner changed. 'Colin, I heard a radio bulletin about this man Carter — '

'He's mine,' he confirmed. Mary had been a cop's wife long enough to know what that meant. 'I'll try and be home some time tonight, once I've done this for Phil. But it depends what happens.'

He said goodbye, hung up, and decided for the tenth time in as many weeks that he was going to have to think about buying another car. There was just the minor detail of finding the money . . .

3

Two weary-looking pressmen and a small black dog prowled the pavement outside the Hydrostat factory, where a uniformed constable stood guard by the main gateway. Colin Thane left the duty car, nodded to the constable, shook his head at the reporters' questions, and went on into the building while the car drove off.

Another constable was stationed in the corridor in the upper floor office area, leaning in bored, time-killing fashion against the wall outside Carter's room. Thane cleared his throat softly, and grinned a little as the man shot upright.

'Where's Sergeant MacLeod?'

'Round the plant somewhere, sir,' said the man hastily. 'He told me to keep an eye on things here. The door's locked, but — '

Thane nodded. 'You can stand down now. Tell him I'm here and that I'll see him soon.'

As the constable went off, another door opened further along the corridor and Jane Maulden emerged, a notebook in one hand, a busy, slightly angry air about her walk.

Thane greeted her as she approached. 'Has

61

David Stanley arrived yet?'

'Oh — ' she blinked, as if noticing him for the first time. 'He's in Mr Hayston's room — I'm on my way there now.'

'Fine.' He followed her along the corridor. The works manager's office was at the very end of its reach, the door lying open, the air inside blue with cigarette smoke. David Stanley lounged in a chair beside the works manager's desk, Hayston stood beside him, and there were two strangers seated opposite.

Peter Hayston saw Thane first, and whispered quickly to his bearded director. Stanley looked up, rose, and came quickly across the room.

'We're just finishing, Thane — give me a moment, will you?' He'd changed his clothes since the morning for a conventional grey business suit with a white shirt and black mourning tie. Hayston, too, had mustered a black tie from somewhere. Stanley beckoned the girl. 'Jane, never mind the notebook. I want you to take care of Mr Shaw — he's joining the firm as of now.'

The younger of the two strangers, a redhead with a long-jawed, wide-mouthed face, rose quickly to his feet.

'Fix him up in the usual way,' instructed Stanley. 'I'll put through salary details and the rest later — oh, and have Danny Benson take him round the plant. He may as well see what goes on.'

For an instant the girl's face showed a mixture of surprise and what might have been sheer indecision. Then she nodded.

'Thanks, Mr Stanley. I appreciate it, with all the other things you've got happening.' Shaw's accent was Scottish, but with a soft Canadian overlay, and the dark brown suit he was wearing hadn't been cut on the European side of the Atlantic.

Stanley waved his thanks aside. 'The job has to keep going, Ian, and you're the man we need. Just look around, find out where things are, and I'll see you later. Any problems till then, ask Jane.'

'Fine.' The new recruit inspected Jane Maulden in unconcealed admiration. 'A pleasure.'

'If you'll come with me.' There were ice-flecks in her voice. Without waiting, she turned with a swing of her raven-dark hair and went out. Shaw grinned around once more, then hurried after her, closing the door behind him as he left.

'Now then, let's see — ' David Stanley broke the temporary silence in the room. 'You've met Hayston. This other character is our public relations expert.'

'Bart Kelly.' The second stranger, middle-aged, vaguely in need of a shave, introduced himself. Grey-haired, pale-faced but alert, he came briskly across the room his hand outstretched. 'Short for Bartholomew, and blame that on my old mother.'

They shook hands. Average height, average build, quietly dressed, Kelly beamed cheerfully. Thane raised an eyebrow. 'Public relations? I thought most of the equipment made here was supposed to be kept out of print.'

Kelly chuckled. 'Now and again I come in handy. But I don't belong to this outfit. I run an industrial publicity and advertising agency, shoestring style.'

'A pretty thick shoestring,' declared Stanley sardonically. 'You've a dozen or more firms on contract, and you're servicing them for fees one stage short of robbery.'

'A fool and his money are soon parted,' countered Kelly serenely. 'That's what my old mother always taught me.'

Behind them, Hayston cleared his throat anxiously. 'Maybe the Chief Inspector wants to talk to you alone, Mr Stanley — '

'Do you?' asked Stanley.

'That depends,' said Thane. 'We need that full statement I mentioned, but if you're going back to see Mrs Carter — '

'Within the hour,' nodded Stanley.

'Then it can wait.'

'Good.' Stanley showed relief. 'This is pretty much of an emergency session, Thane. Remember those car tests I told you about?'

'The Ministry series?'

'The same. Well, with Bill Carter dead and all that means, I telephoned and tried to get a week's postponement.' Stanley shrugged. 'They said no. It has to be this week, or we wait months until they can set things up again.' He paused, as if to let the words sink in. 'I don't like having to do this, but it's vital we go ahead. That's why I had Bart come over - afterwards I'm hoping we'll manage some skeleton of a press release that won't offend the Defence people. Then there could be technical press statements, advertising and — '

'And plenty more,' agreed Kelly. 'Anyway, I've heard all I need to know about arrangements. I can call you back later if there are problems.'

'You handle all the firm's publicity material?' queried Thane.

'The lot,' said Kelly. 'Bill Carter signed me on soon after he got started.' His face clouded. 'A pal of mine on the *Evening View* phoned me this morning and told me what had happened — it took a lot of believing.'

'Newspapers — ' Hayston was polishing the thick lenses of his spectacles on the end of his tie. He gave a shudder at the word. 'I don't know how many calls we've had today — I finally told the switchboard to stop accepting them.'

'Just give them a straight 'no comment',' advised Kelly. 'Say anything else, and they can make a meal of it.'

David Stanley fidgeted impatiently. 'What about you, Chief Inspector? Any questions we can answer?'

'A couple,' agreed Thane amiably. 'You've had time to check through the safe contents and the rest of your records?'

'With your sergeant breathing down my neck.' Stanley scowled at the memory. 'If there's anything missing I can't spot it. The same with his desk.'

'What about the desk drawer where the key broke off?'

'Personal stuff, pencils, a railway timetable.' Stanley took out his cigarettes and lit one with frowning concentration. 'He could have broken the key himself, anytime, for all I know. But there's nothing missing — and your own people say there's no sign of any attempt to force the safe.'

'Doesn't make much sense, does it?' commented Kelly wryly. 'I was asking if

— well, say it was somebody on the prowl for more than ordinary burglary reasons, whether he couldn't find out plenty from just looking around the plant, or maybe taking some pictures.'

'Not unless he was a trained engineer with a squad of men to help him strip units down, measure their components and reassemble them,' snapped Stanley. One large hand swept the idea aside. 'Anyway, leave that sort of thing to the police. Right, Thane?'

'We prefer it that way.' Thane rubbed his chin reflectively. 'One thing we're checking on is the distribution of keys to the plant. Where were yours, Mr Stanley?'

'With me — and that means in Switzerland.' Stanley took a stance near the window. 'Now you can help me. It's about Bill Carter — there won't be a release of his body for burial for some days, right?'

'It depends on the medical people,' said Thane cautiously. 'They might give a release after a week, but it could be longer.'

'I'm glad,' declared Stanley. He thumbed towards Hayston with brief impatience. 'Our works manager doesn't like the idea of business as usual — but I've the long-term situation, the firm's future, to consider. That's one reason why I'm hiring this new boy, Ian Shaw. We need an extra man now on the team going north for the trials.'

'From his voice I'd label him Scots-Canadian, probably more Scots than the rest,' said Thane. He'd been coming round to ask about Shaw anyway, remembering the Maulden girl's strange reaction.

'Born here, left about seven years ago, emigrated to Canada and worked on hydrostatic projects in the Toronto area,' summarised Stanley briefly. 'He came back to tidy up some family business — and he happens to be a highly qualified technician.'

'A lucky find.'

Stanley nodded. 'But the credit's Hayston's, not mine.'

'Well . . . ' Peter Hayston flushed at being the centre of attention. 'Shaw came in last week looking for a job. I passed him in to Mr Carter, and he interviewed him and told him to come back today — '

'We've got him and that's what matters,' growled Stanley brusquely. 'While you're here, Thane, you'd better know we plan to leave the city tomorrow night, heading north. The Ministry tests begin first thing on Wednesday, around the Lochalsh area.'

The news made Thane wince. Such an early move was just about the last thing he wanted, yet in the circumstances and with such strong Government interest there was little he could do to prevent it.

'Well, any police objections?' queried Stanley.

'Not as long as we know where to contact you.' Thane glanced at his watch then began heading for the door. 'I've a sergeant on the loose outside — I'd better find out what he's doing.'

Bart Kelly grinned as the door swung open. 'Don't fancy a trip north with us, Chief Inspector?'

Thane stopped, looked at the three men quietly, and saw their expressions gradually change as they waited for his answer.

'It might come to that,' he said softly. 'You can never tell, Mr Kelly. But if I make that kind of trip it won't be for anyone's pleasure.'

Silenced, Kelly glanced at the others. David Stanley's mouth had clamped shut, Hayston began rubbing one hand quickly and nervously against the other.

Thane nodded and went out, closing the door behind him. He waited outside and gave a brief, wintry smile as, at last, the voices began.

His next stop was just along the corridor, at Jane Maulden's office. He gave a light tap on the door and went in.

'Looking for someone, Chief Inspector?' She had been working at her desk, but she pushed the bundle of papers aside and greeted him with a slightly wan smile.

'I've found her.' Thane perched himself on the edge of the desk opposite and returned the smile. 'Like to help me sort out a few problems?'

'Go ahead,' she invited, showing immediate interest.

'Yourself first. How long have you been private secretary to both partners?'

'Just over two years.'

'Like the job — until this happened, I mean?'

She nodded 'Very much. And' — twin patches of colour flared to life in her cheeks — 'well, there was more to it than just a good pay packet.'

'Was?'

'Mr Carter knew my father — they worked together once. That's why he gave me the job.'

'And you liked him?'

'Yes.' Her head snapped up. 'As a family friend, Chief Inspector, nothing more.'

'That's all I meant,' soothed Thane. 'Jane, how did he get on with David Stanley?'

'Very well.' She answered quickly, almost too quickly.

'No quarrels, no disagreements?'

'Sometimes they saw things differently,' she

70

admitted. 'But neither of them went into a huff about it.'

He nodded. 'And Mrs Carter?'

She gave him a duplicate of the frozen look he'd seen directed at young Shaw earlier. 'I don't know what you mean.'

'Lynne Carter is the third director,' he said patiently. 'Whose side did she take when there was a row going on?'

'It wasn't my business to find out, Chief Inspector.'

He sighed. 'Being loyal, Jane?'

'Being truthful, Chief Inspector.' She glanced away from him for a moment, gnawing lightly on her lower lip. 'I — there is something else, though.'

He raised an eyebrow but didn't speak, letting the girl set her own pace, sensing her unhappy reluctance.

'There was a man who left as you came in — '

'Ian Shaw?' Thane nodded. 'I'm told he's joining the test team.'

'Yes, as a driver-mechanic.' Her left hand strayed to the neck of her dress, and Colin Thane noticed the engagement finger was bare. 'He's been here before, more than once.' She took a deep breath. 'The last time was Friday afternoon, and he must have arrived during the lunch hour. I came back a

71

little early, and I was going to go into Mr Carter's office to tidy his desk. But — well, they were there, Ian Shaw and Mr Carter. They were arguing, and Shaw was angry, really angry.'

'Could you hear what they were saying?'

She shook her head. 'No, just their voices and how they sounded. That was enough.'

Thane pursed his lips, trying to fit what she was telling him into some place in the pattern. 'You're sure it was Shaw? Did you go into the room?'

'No, I came back in here. But then I heard Mr Carter's door open then slam shut again. I — I deliberately started out into the corridor again, and this man Shaw barged past. He nearly knocked me down.'

'Did he say anything?'

'I — I don't think he really knew I was there.'

'And Mr Carter?'

Again she shook her head. 'He rang for me a little later, and dictated some letters. But he didn't mention anyone having been with him.' She hesitated, worry in her eyes. 'I'm not saying he necessarily had anything to do with Mr Carter being killed — '

'But he's worth finding out about,' mused Thane.

She reached into the top drawer of her desk

and brought out a small buff card. 'This is his personnel card. I can type another one.'

'Good.' Thane slipped the card into his pocket. 'I'll let you know what happens.' As he went out, he heard her give a long sigh.

Detective Sergeant MacLeod took a little finding, but at last Thane located him prowling around one of the small machine shops on the west side of the ground floor.

'Nothing much to tell, sir,' reported MacLeod gloomily. 'Either everyone has been spinning me the same line, or this place is the original big happy family.'

'No dislikes? Not even a leaky roof or a row over bonus rates?'

MacLeod shuffled his feet unhappily. 'Nothing, unless the way they feel about this works manager fellow Hayston. Even then, it's just that they treat him as pretty much of a joke.'

'You've got his statement and the same from the keyholders on the staff?'

'The head foreman?' MacLeod nodded. 'He's an old-timer named Benson — seems straight enough.'

'There's a new fellow starting, Mac. His name is Shaw, Ian Shaw — keep an eye on him.'

'Sir?' MacLeod was puzzled. 'You mean I've to stay here?'

'Till the place closes for the night, yes.'
Thane grinned unsympathetically. 'Then you
can follow Shaw home.' He turned to leave
then changed his mind and beckoned
MacLeod to come with him. 'While I'm here,
let's have another look at that safe in Carter's
room.'

MacLeod followed him back along the
corridors, up the stairway, and produced the
key which unlocked Carter's door. Inside the
room the safe was lying open, exposing an
unexpectedly vast amount of space within.
But most of the metal shelves were empty.

'Scientific Bureau checked everything first,
sir,' explained MacLeod warily. 'Then I had
Mr Stanley make his own examination to
confirm nothing was missing. After that
— well, most of the stuff was needed for
production work.'

'Fair enough.' Thane frowned at the twin
dials, one for the combination lock, the other
for the time lock. They reminded him vaguely
of a new eye-level oven Mary had wanted
when they redecorated the kitchen. Not that
she'd got it — the kids had needed new
outfits for school.

He sighed and stood back. 'Superintendent
Laurence is coming out to look this over.'

'Any idea why, sir?'

'No.' Thane gave a brief, whimsical

grimace. 'The back-room brigade like to keep their little secrets — at least till they're sure there's no chance of mistake.'

He left the factory a few minutes later, talked cheerfully and determinedly about the weather to the two sentinel pressmen, then hailed a passing taxi and climbed aboard.

The ride back to Millside gave him time to think — not that it helped much. There were too many angles, too few facts in the whole situation. And this latest, the strange business of Ian Shaw having a row with Carter then happily taking a job with Carter's firm the same day the latter was found murdered, was as strange as any.

He grimaced, abandoned speculation, and set his mind to listing what had to be done. That, at least, would have won Superintendent Donfoot's approval.

★　★　★

The clock in the outer office was ticking towards 4 p.m. when Colin Thane left the taxi and walked into the Millside Division building. Upstairs, in the C.I.D. section, typewriters were pecking at a slow pace. Some of the day shift were doing report sheets, and taking their time about it. They were due off when the clock reached the hour and the evening team began arriving — until then, report sheets were a useful way of avoiding more strenuous possibilities.

Thane's eyes twinkled, remembering when he'd played the same 'look busy' game. But halfway across the room a figure suddenly rose and barred his way.

'Sir — ' Detective Constable Beech, usually a difficult young man to find when wanted, was anxious to be finished and gone.

'Well?'

'I put a visitor in your office, Chief Inspector — he's from Admiralty security. And Inspector Moss telephoned in. He said to tell you he's making progress and he hopes tonight's arrangement still stands.'

'Does he?' Thane inspected the young D.C. with deliberate care. 'How about you, Beech? In any rush to get home?'

'Eh . . . ' Beech took a moment to recover. 'Well, I do have plans, sir.'

'Here's something you can do first. Get on to Immigration, and find out when an Ian Shaw returned to this country from Canada.' Thane brought the Hydrostat Drives personnel card from his pocket and handed it over. 'This may help. And Beech — '

'Sir?' D.C. Beech swallowed his despair.

'Don't take too long, will you?' Thane's mouth twitched a little as his victim headed unhappily towards the nearest telephone. Then he remembered the waiting Admiralty man, his face hardened, and he walked slowly towards his room, ready to do battle.

The man standing by the window turned as the door clicked open. He laid a brown leather briefcase against the sill and smiled.

'Chief Inspector Thane? We spoke by 'phone — I'm Allowes. Glad to meet you.'

Thane's mouth dropped a little in surprise as he closed the door behind him. The voice was the same, but the rest — Commander Allowes was a fat little butterball of a man with the mild face of a parish priest and the sober, city-styled apparel of a promotion-seeking bank manager. His eyes were a pale, watery blue, the hand he extended was small and podgy, and its grip was a mere thistledown of a touch.

'I'm afraid we rather annoyed you this morning,' said the Admiralty man in the crisp, clipped accent so oddly at variance with his appearance.

'Morning isn't my best time for manners.' Thane treated his visitor with an inbred, polite caution. 'Sit down, won't you?'

'Stay on my feet if you don't mind.' Commander Allowes padded back towards the window. 'Spend too much of my life now on my backside — with my build that's fatal.'

He turned, his face losing a little of its mild pleasance. 'Any further forward with the Carter business?'

'Not much.' Thane tossed his hat on its peg behind the door and joined Allowes by the window. Dark, heavy rain clouds were building up again to the west, heading fast towards the city. A rainstorm was about all he needed to complete his day. 'We're finding it rough going.'

'An honest man — thank heaven for that, anyway!' Allowes laughed, but the watery blue eyes showed little mirth. 'Well, I brought our screening records on the factory personnel. And now I'm here seems as good a time as any to tell you a little more. We're fairly positive there's an information leakage out of Hydrostat Drives.'

Thane felt as if an icy chill had touched against him. 'Fairly positive?'

The Admiralty man sighed. 'Plain and simply positive, if you prefer it, Chief Inspector. London received a little package of film out of Cairo a few days back — how the pictures were taken isn't my business. For all I know somebody disguised himself as a camel for the day. But we've some crystal-clear close-ups taken aboard one of the newest Soviet guided missile destroyers when it was paying a courtesy call on the U.A.R.

78

They include a couple of shots of hydrostatic drive gadgets which Carter's firm only turned out in prototype a few months back.'

'Couldn't they have developed their own equipment, independently?' For Thane, the question held little hope.

'Not a chance. We're an estimated eighteen months ahead of them on hydrostatic research.' Allowes shrugged, and his whole body seemed to quiver. 'Frankly, I don't care who kills who in civvy street, Thane. That's your worry. But if it ever came to what's vulgarly termed the crunch, it would be downright embarrassing to know that what little is left of the Royal Navy was liable to be sunk with the help of some of our own secret goodies. Don't you agree?'

Thane nodded. What had once been a vague shadow of a nightmare was now a cold, hard reality.

'Ah, well, that's life.' The fat security man fished into a pocket, pulled out a small paper bag, and thrust it forward. 'Like a peppermint, Chief Inspector?'

A double whisky would have suited better. But Thane took one of the round white lumps and sucked on it dolefully.

'The problem now is whether Carter's death is linked to the security aspect or stands separate,' mused Allowes. 'While I was waiting I — ah — took the liberty of looking at your case file.' He shook his head reproachfully. 'It's empty.'

Thane glanced at his desk, remembered the folder prepared by Phil Moss, and grunted. 'We've been busy.'

'Quite.' Allowes was sympathetic. 'That — ah — envelope in your tray is the post mortem report. I collected it at the mortuary on my way here.'

'Thanks very much,' said Thane dryly. He crossed over, slit the envelope open, and scanned the close-typed sheets it contained.

There was the usual formal preamble that the information was prepared 'on soul and conscience' by Doc Williams and Professor MacMaster, and that it was a preliminary summary with more to follow.

'You were interested in the blood group, I believe,' said Allowes, still standing by the window. 'The report says he was Group O.'

'We found traces of Group B,' said Thane briefly. 'Nasal blood — it could have happened in a struggle.' He edged down into his chair, still reading.

On the subject of general examination the summary was suitably precise.

Carter's body showed no trace of wounds beyond minor bruising on the left lower jaw, a slight cut on his inner lower lip and an equally slight graze on his forehead.

'Death was due to heat apoplexy, the result of prolonged exposure to abnormally high temperature.' But as for the time of death — Thane cursed softly as he struggled with the cautious verbiage. Possibilities and probabilities, 'unknown extraneous factors' and 'loose speculation approximations' there seemed no end to the hedging operation being carried out by the two pathologists. Only the final paragraphs held a grain of hope.

'Due to the presence of a degree of heat stiffening, the result of coagulation of albuminates in the muscles, the normal factor of rigor mortis did not supervene.

'But a light meal of breakfast cereal had been consumed some seven or nine hours before death. This combined with the degree of hypostasis staining present in the body tissue allows a present belief, subject to the results of more detailed investigation, that death might have occurred some time between mid-afternoon and mid-evening on Sunday.'

It wasn't much, but it was a start. He quietly folded the report and slipped it into the Carter file.

'This is yours, too — on unofficial and purely temporary loan, of course.'

He looked up. Commander Allowes' briefcase was open and the Admiralty man had extracted a thick quarto-size envelope.

'The Hydrostat Drive personnel detail,' said Allowes. He laid the envelope on Thane's desk and refastened the case. 'Incidentally, we advised the firm quite recently that we weren't too happy about their overall security — but at the time we weren't sure enough of our ground to say more. Ah — anything else you need from me?'

'There may be, later,' said Thane grimly. 'You know they start a series of Ministry vehicle tests on Wednesday? According to Stanley, they can't win a postponement.'

Allowes gave a cluck of surprise. 'That's awkward — still, couldn't your people make some kind of order?'

'So far we've no strong enough reason to force them to stay.'

'True.' Allowes glanced at his watch. 'It's a little early to offer you a gin to go with that peppermint, Thane. But I imagine we'll have other opportunities.' He nodded, and began heading for the door.

'Commander — ' Thane stopped him, a baffled curiosity in his voice. 'What do you think happened?'

'I haven't the slightest idea. I'm rather hoping you'll find out.' The Admiralty man's genial mask stayed in place. 'But you know, there's just a chance all this might end up with our killing several birds with one stone.'

The fat, almost comical figure was gone from the room before Thane had time to say more.

★ ★ ★

The threatened rainstorm broke at six and Phil Moss arrived wet, weary, yet oddly triumphant about an hour later.

By then, the Carter file had, at last, begun to assume respectable proportions. By telephone and teletype, by holding on to the reluctant D.C. Beech, by diverting three of the evening shift team from less important routine, by driving himself as hard as any of the rest, Colin Thane had gathered up most of the loose threads that existed.

Immigration had reported that Ian Shaw, aged twenty-four, occupation research engineer, had entered the United Kingdom from Canada via Prestwick Airport a month earlier. The airline concerned, Air Canada, confirmed — and added the intriguing fact that Shaw, flying over on a twenty-one day economy return, had within two weeks of his arrival asked for a refund on the return half of his ticket. He planned on staying longer than he'd anticipated.

Continental Trunks checked records and agreed that a person-to-person call had been made late on the Saturday night from Carter's home to David Stanley at the latter's hotel near Lucerne. It had lasted six minutes. A teletype from the Interpol clearing house at Geneva reported that Stanley had been a last-minute passenger aboard a B.E.A. flight which left Basle for London early the next morning.

There was less to go on when it came to Lynne Carter. Subscriber trunk dialling ruled out any possibility of tracing the call from her husband. The sleek Bayswater hotel where she'd been staying, visited by London Metropolitan detectives, recalled a telephone call being put through to her room late on the Saturday night. Their accounts file had a record of her checking out at mid-morning on the Sunday. The Metropolitan teletype expanded a little on what had happened.

'Subject advised her departure at breakfast, was joined shortly after by man described as tall, bearded, heavily built, casually dressed. They departed together in subject's Alfa Romeo car shortly before 11 a.m.'

Thane pencilled a calculation on the margin of the message form. London to

Glasgow was four hundred miles. Give a moderate average speed of forty m.p.h., add time for meal stops on the way . . . he ringed the figures, put a heavy question mark beside them, and got down to the next item, the Hydrostat factory file.

When Admiralty security did a screening job they were thorough, the result of past and bitter experience. Two of the older employees were listed as one-time members of the Party, but it was an affiliation which had ended long years ago, when the once Red Clydeside began to realise there were other things in life than an ambition to lynch capitalists from lamp-posts. They were classified as 'A.1 risk' — and so, with minor comments in a handful of cases, were the rest of the sixty or so workers.

He put a few sheets to one side.

Peter Hayston . . . 'works manager, aged twenty-nine, single, nervous disposition. Underwent six month hospital rehabilitation for alcoholism at age of twenty. Strong personal loyalty vouched for by director W. Carter, with whom worked for period prior to company's formation.'

Jane Maulden . . . 'private secretary, aged twenty-four, single, good family background, won university scholarship award, holidays abroad but contacts satisfactory.'

David Stanley . . . 'company director, aged thirty-eight, divorced, held rank of captain in Royal Artillery, decorated for bravery Korea, two convictions for violence Glasgow.'

And finally, there was Carter . . . 'Athletic background, fringe interest in Peace Front movement ended at time of Hungarian uprising. Built up career from engineer apprentice, tendency to overwork.'

Most of it he'd either known or could have guessed. But they made handy confirmation, cut corners, saved time.

An orderly delivered a brief note from the Scientific Bureau, but it was restricted to what Dan Laurence had already given him verbally.

The uniformed branch weighed in with the results of interviewing beat men who'd been on patrol near the factory during the weekend. One constable had noticed lights burning in the office section on the Saturday evening. The next time he'd passed, about 10 p.m., Carter had been leaving the building . . . most of the beat men knew Carter from his habit of walking where other people would have used car or bus.

Thane had opened a new pack of cigarettes and was starting on his third mug of tea when Moss slouched in. Water dripped from the Millside second-in-command's hat and from

86

the point of his nose, and the shoulders of his coat were black with rain.

'Welcome back to the Ark.' Thane shoved the pack across his desk. Moss first dried one hand on his shirt front then took a cigarette, accepted a light, and grumbled his way into a chair.

'Still wet outside?' queried Thane.

The reply was short, terse, and unlikely to be found in any standard glossary of Scottish folk phrases.

Thane chuckled. 'All right, how'd you make out?'

'Not bad.' Moss took off his hat and slapped the worst of the rainwater from its brim. 'Carter's neighbours were useful. One of them went round to the house late on Saturday — he knew Carter was on his own and wanted to invite him round for supper. Carter cut him off short and seemed worried as hell about something. A couple of others saw him leave home on the Sunday morning about eleven. Nobody saw him come back.'

'Any visitors?'

'None that we know about.' Moss grimaced. 'But I located the local gossip, an old crone with time on her hands. According to her, our blonde Mrs Carter is no angel. Sometimes Carter had to go away on business trips, and Lady Lynne didn't believe in moping at home.'

'Men?'

'Mainly in the singular — David Stanley.'

Thane felt no particular surprise. 'He told me he was going back out there this afternoon.'

Moss nodded. 'He arrived just as I finished getting Mrs Carter's statement.'

'Their stories match?'

'Like a duet. They left her hotel about 11 a.m., did about thirty miles, then Stanley had a notion to look at some mountain roads in North Wales on the way up — he thought they might make a good test circuit for the experimental vehicles. They 'phoned Carter at home, caught him just about to go out — he didn't say where — and told him what they were doing. It was evening by the time they'd finished exploring around Wales and they got back here a little after nine this morning.'

Thane snorted. 'What did they do — walk back? I've done from here to North Wales in ten hours, and that's with the family loaded aboard.'

'They had engine trouble,' said Moss, his face expressionless, his voice cynical. 'Carburettors, to be exact. Stanley did a repair job by the roadside, but they still had to nurse the car the rest of the way.'

'Engine trouble.' Thane gave an incredulous growl. 'What about food, fuel? They'd have to stop somewhere on a five-hundred-mile outing.'

'Packed meals from the hotel, and they filled a couple of reserve jerricans that just happened to be in the car.' Moss leaned forward and stubbed the cigarette on an ashtray. 'Well, it's original anyway — and Stanley showed me a stack of notes he says he made when they were travelling over this new test route.'

'Which he could probably have surveyed any time in the last year or so.' Thane's fingers beat a slow tattoo on the desk. 'That's all they can offer? They didn't see anyone, speak to anyone?'

'Not the way they tell it.'

'Great!' As an alibi it was madness. But they both knew that the crazier an alibi the more it was dangerously likely to be true. 'All right, we'll take them up on it, Phil. Find the garage that services her car. If she puts it in for repair I want to know what was wrong with the carburettors. And teleprint right down the line, all county forces they'd pass through. Maybe somebody noticed them.'

'Right.' Moss rose to his feet. 'Eh . . . anything else right now?' He tried to make his voice sound unconcerned.

'Better give Doc Williams a call while you're at it,' remembered Thane. 'He wants to talk to you.'

'And after that?'

Thane chuckled and gave in. 'Emma Robertson's, you piece of chronic misery.'

Moss relaxed with a sigh.

★ ★ ★

The place Phil Moss called home was an old two-storey villa on the south side of the river, in the Pollokshields district. Once, close to the turn of the century, Sunfarne Street had been labelled 'select,' each house with its own tethering blocks, horse carriages, white-aproned maids to polish the brass doorpulls, and discreet rear-lane tradesmen's entrances.

But now, as the Millside duty car approached through the steadily falling rain, wipers slapping, tyres hissing over the water-filmed tarmac, Sunfarne Street presented a very different picture. Even the combination of late dusk and the soft glow of old-fashioned street lamps couldn't completely hide the long grass and weeds in neglected gardens, the sagging fences, the way in which all but a few of the once grand houses were now in considerable need of paint and repair.

The black Jaguar stopped briefly at the pavement's edge and the uniformed driver grinned as he watched his two passengers make a fast sprint through the downpour towards the villa's porch.

Thane made it first, then had to wait, cursing the dribbling leaks from the cracked, warped roof. Moss used his key, the door swung open, they moved quickly inside.

'Now what?' queried Thane as the door creaked shut again.

Moss looked around the narrow, oak-panelled hallway with its potted plants and old-fashioned coat-stand. All was quiet.

'Upstairs — to my place,' he decided in a hoarse attempt at a whisper.

Thane followed him up the long stairway, covered in worn grey carpet. On the upper floor, the main furnishing on the landing was a large glass tank with half a dozen fat, complacent goldfish nosing around in its depths.

Phil Moss occupied the best of Emma Robertson's upstairs rooms, with a small and seldom-used kitchen attached. Once inside he tossed his hat on a table, dumped his coat over the back of the nearest chair and then, as Thane followed his example, glanced briefly at a couple of envelopes propped on the mantelshelf above the room's electric fire.

'Bills,' he said briefly, triggering the fire's switch with one flick of his foot. 'Let's have some light, Colin.'

Thane nodded, found the light switch, and the big, shaded centre bulb came to life.

'Like a beer?' Moss leaned over the back of the bed settee and produced a couple of bottles. He prised the caps off against a corner of the mantelshelf, located glasses among a confusion of oddments in the top drawer of his dressing chest, and began pouring. All around, the room showed traces of the constant battle between its occupant's untidy self and his landlady's determined attentions.

'Thanks.' Thane took his glass. 'Well, when do we talk to her?'

'She'll know we're in.' Moss sipped his beer, then, as if avoiding what lay ahead, announced, 'Doc Williams wants me to go and see someone.'

'Ulcer-wise?'

Moss nodded. 'Some quack with a new treatment — no diet, no knife-work.' He belched politely. 'All he does is stick needles in you.'

'I'll do that any time, for free — ' Thane broke off as he heard a brief tap on the room door. He glanced at Moss, took a long swallow at his beer, and stood ready.

'Good evening, Philip — and you're here, too, Mr Thane!' Emma Robertson beamed as she came into the room. She was a plump little woman, tightly corseted, her greying hair neatly brush-waved, a neat floral smock covering her pale blue dress. 'Now then, you'll be wanting something to eat, eh?'

'We can't stay long,' warned Thane. 'We've still work to do.'

'A case?' She pronounced it in capital letters and nodded wisely. 'Well, I've got some nice fresh sea trout all ready to be grilled. Five minutes?'

'Grand, Mrs Robertson.' Moss shifted awkwardly. 'I was telling Mr Thane your news.'

She giggled as if thirty years younger. 'Marrying again at my age — and he probably thinks I'm daft, eh?'

'I wouldn't say that,' protested Thane gallantly. 'Just as long as you've known the man long enough and — well, you know what I mean.'

'We only met a few weeks ago, when I was down south on holiday,' she admitted cheerfully. 'But Arthur and I — Arthur Clark, he's an engraver — '

'I know.'

'Oh?' She showed surprise.

'Phil told me,' explained Thane hastily.

'Of course!' She beamed again. 'Arthur and I feel it seems much longer.'

'You'll keep the boarding house?'

'No, Arthur says I've to stop working.' She glanced around the room, frowned, and crossed to tidy a jumble of magazines lying near the window. 'I'll miss my boarders, of course. But I can see Arthur's point of view. Properly invested, the money would bring in quite a nice return.'

Thane winced. 'That depends on the investment, Mrs Robertson.'

'Oh, but Arthur — ' she stopped, looked at Thane closely, then gave a chuckle. 'I see. You're worried in case I'm making a fool of myself. If I know Philip, he's probably making noises like a policeman and trying to find out all he can about Arthur.'

'Well — ' Moss swallowed weakly.

'I thought so.' She gave Moss an affectionate pat on the arm. 'But you needn't have worried. When it comes to money, I never do anything without asking my lawyer.'

'And the lucky bridegroom?' queried Thane. 'Is this his first marriage?'

'No,' admitted the widow calmly. 'But he's just waiting for his divorce to become final. His wife ran off with a sailor and left the poor soul on his own.' She bustled around the room, collected the two empty beer bottles, and sighed at the rest. 'Now, I'll go and see to your fish — they won't take long.'

Neither man spoke until she'd gone.

'You didn't get very far,' declared Moss bitterly.

'I didn't,' admitted Thane. 'But I know this much, Phil. The only way to convince her that Splits Clark is on the crook is to let her find out for herself.'

'And how the devil do we do that?' growled Moss.

Thane shrugged. 'I'll work on it.'

Emma Robertson brought their meal to the room as she'd promised, but stayed only a moment.

'I'm meeting Arthur,' she explained blithely.

Thane sighed to himself, then concentrated on the plate laid before him. The sea trout were fat, succulent, beautifully grilled. If Splits Clark pulled this off he was on a good thing in more ways than one.

★ ★ ★

As they'd arranged, the duty car returned to the house within the hour. The rain showed no sign of letting up, and they dashed through it to the Jaguar's opened rear door, tumbled in, then realised that someone else was already aboard.

'Dirty night, sir.' Detective Sergeant MacLeod, sitting in front beside the driver, sniffed reproachfully at the spectacle of his two superior officers sprawled wet and well-fed on the leather upholstery.

'Mac, what the devil brings you here?' demanded Thane.

'Maybe he likes the company,' volunteered Moss, wiping crumbs from around his mouth. 'I thought you said he was sticking with Shaw.'

MacLeod was hurt. 'It's coming on for nine o'clock, Chief Inspector,' he said pointedly. By his reckoning, divisional chiefs and their immediate deputies might be paid to work round the clock. But he had a wife at home who didn't feel the same applied on a sergeant's pay. 'I've had one of the night team take over. And I thought you'd better know Superintendent Laurence wants you to meet him at Carter's factory.'

'Now?' Thane raised an eyebrow. 'All right.'

Their driver looked round, caught Thane's nod, and slid the car into gear.

'Let's hear about Shaw,' suggested Thane as the car pulled away, rain almost drowning the noise of its engine. 'In brief, Mac.'

MacLeod settled himself more comfortably, one arm draped along the back of his seat. 'He explored around the Hydrostat building until it closed at five, then left like the rest — he's driving a black Volkswagen. I followed him out to that new motel place near Barlinnie Prison. One of the cabins is rented in his name.'

'Handy,' murmured Moss.

MacLeod suffered the interruption without comment. 'He stayed there long enough to have a meal and change his clothes. When he left, he drove back into the city, parked the Volkswagen near Central Station and went into a bar in Hope Street.' He paused for effect. 'That's where he met Peter Hayston.'

'Their works manager?' Thane swore softly and leaned forward. 'You're sure, Mac?'

'I kept well back,' admitted MacLeod. 'But my eyesight's good enough and you know the way Hayston dresses.'

Thane frowned through the window at the dark, rain-washed roadway. 'That's something I hadn't expected.'

MacLeod shrugged. 'Hayston arrived a minute or two after Shaw. They went straight over to a table and talked for a spell, then Hayston went out.'

'New boy buys the boss a drink,' murmured Moss. 'Well, it isn't a crime — just unlikely. How did they act, Mac?'

'Friendly enough at first,' said MacLeod.

'But Shaw didn't seem very happy by the time they'd finished.' He took two cigarettes from the pack Thane offered, lit one for himself, and passed the other to their driver.

'Anything more?' asked Thane, settling back.

'Not much, sir.' MacLeod drew briefly on his cigarette. 'Shaw left the bar soon after Hayston had gone. He drove straight back to the motel. Once he seemed settled, I asked the night shift to take over.'

Moss grunted. 'With luck he'll be there for the night. Anyone roaming around in weather like this needs his head examined.'

Colin Thane sat silent for a spell, watching the street lights flicker past. The burly Millside chief had an uneasy feeling that the night's surprises were far from over and that Dan Laurence's summons might mean another unexpected turn. There was a growing tiredness in his mind and he felt he needed a shave, wanted one, however irrational it might seem.

'Colin?' Moss's elbow nudged against his side.

'Sorry.' He forced a grin, rubbed his hand briskly across the back of his neck to chase some of the tension from his system, and felt better. 'One thing's certain, Phil. I want to know more about young Ian Shaw. Like why he flies in from Canada on a round-trip ticket, then decides to stay.'

'Maybe that's how he wanted it to look from the start,' suggested Moss.

'Maybe, or maybe something made him change his mind,' said Thane softly. 'We're going to have to find out.'

4

When Dan Laurence loosened his tie and got down to his shirt sleeves it was a sure sign that the Scientific Bureau were up to their own highly technical brand of fun. A cigarette drooping from his lips, his white hair in rumpled confusion, Superintendent Laurence sat on a small folding stool beside the opened safe door in Carter's office. A three-bar portable lighting rig poured its glare over one shoulder. Two of his inevitable aides stood ready with a collection of fine-bladed instruments, slapped as required into Laurence's open hand in the same way as a surgeon might receive a scalpel.

Given some theatre masks and the background hiss of a steriliser the picture would have been complete. But a mask would have prevented Dan smoking, and the type of operation was one in which the Bureau chief's heavy, almost asthmatic breathing was almost the only sound to disturb the silence.

He stopped as he heard footsteps in the factory corridor, then gave a grunt which dislodged the cigarette's ash.

'Aye, you took your time coming,' he

accused the new arrivals.

'Mac had to find us first,' soothed Thane, leading the Millside trio into the room. 'Been busy?'

'Busy?' Laurence growled the word. 'I've been here since the place closed at five. See this safe?' He gestured towards the opened door, the deep interior empty, its normal contents temporarily transferred. 'Steel plating like battleship armour, anti-explosive bolts, a combination lock, then this fancy time lock — aye, an' the lot not worth a twopenny damn!'

Thane crossed over, prepared for the worst. 'What about it, Dan?'

Laurence placed the tips of his fingers together, happy at the chance of lecturing an audience. 'Somebody's been playing clever, Colin. Clever enough to — to fool the brawn brigade like you and MacLeod, or even an old relic like Phil here.'

'Relic?' Moss snorted. 'At least I don't spend my life on my backside, like — '

Thane grinned and waved him down. 'Let him get it over with, Phil. You've got to humour the intellectuals.'

'Humph.' Laurence beckoned them closer. 'Anyway, look at this. First we've a modern four-figure combination lock, standard type. Nothing wrong with it. Then this' — he tapped the time-lock dial on the outer door — 'Swiss made, registers up to one hundred and twenty hours. All you do is set the pointer to the length of time you want to pass before the safe can be opened. You say the plant closed at five on the Friday, an' the safe was set to open at eight on the Monday, correct?'

Thane nodded. 'We've two witnesses.'

'Good.' Laurence glanced at his two assistants and they grinned in unison, anticipating what came next. 'That's a total of sixty-three hours. Now watch.' He spun the dial's knob until it registered the figure, then very deliberately slammed the door shut. A lock clicked.

'But you've — ' Thane stopped, bewildered.

'It shouldn't open for sixty-three hours,' agreed Laurence. 'Try the door.'

Thane tugged the handle. It didn't budge.

'Aye.' Laurence glanced at his big silver pocket watch. 'Now listen, and I'll try to put this in nice, simple language.' His cigarette had burned down almost to lip level. He let it fall to the floor and extinguished it under one heavy foot. 'Time locks have one basic purpose — to make sure that in a place like this, where more than one man has to know the combination key of the main lock, there's still no chance o' the safe being opened outside authorised hours. With the best makes — an' this is one, believe me — they don't take chances. There are four separate clockwork mechanisms working inside the door, all actuated by the outer dial. Even if three o' the clocks break down, the fourth is enough to keep that door locked until the time dialled has expired.'

'Can't you turn the dial back the way, sir?' asked MacLeod earnestly.

'No, you can't.' Laurence sighed. 'How some folk even make sergeant — ach, it beats me. Anyway, there's a steel locking bolt. It thumps out an' engages when the time lock comes into operation. And each one of those four wee clock mechanisms — ' he stopped and grunted. 'Tommy, you take over. It was your idea.'

The nearest of the two Bureau D.C.'s, the man Thane had met that morning, was happy to oblige.

'It started off as a guess,' he confessed. 'Our oil heating at home works through a time switch — nice for having the place warm when we get up. You can set it on a twenty-four hour programme, or use another set of contacts which control over seven days,' A whimsical grimace crossed his face. 'I've had the devil of a job sorting things out when we've gone away for a weekend.'

Thane nodded. He'd once tried to wire a time-switch to a radio, and had blown every fuse they possessed.

'Tommy asked me to take a look at this one,' grunted Laurence. 'The principle's the same. Each clock movement has a small stud. That stud comes round when the time lapse zeroes, the stud triggers a lever, the lever takes tension off the locking bolt, an' the safe can be opened. But remember, only when the stud zeroes.' He glanced at his watch again. 'Now, somebody give me a cigarette while we wait another minute.'

Thane obliged. Laurence scraped a match with his thumbnail, lit the cigarette, and stared fixedly at the safe door.

The click, when it came, was barely audible.

'Colin — '

Thane needed no second invitation. He grabbed the handle, tugged, and the safe door opened with the faintest of squeaks.

'Get at the inside of one of those things an' you've got it licked,' said Laurence happily. 'The crude way is to saw through the retaining lever, but then, if you close the safe and give a wee tug to check, it opens again.'

'The studs?' queried Moss.

'Good,' agreed Laurence in patronising

fashion. He tapped a small, quartered panel on the inside of the door. 'I've taken off a wee glass hatch cover to get at the works o' the thing. Two or three hours toil wi' a watchmaking kit and you could alter one of those stud settings, or rebuild the escapement, so that the clock movement went birling round at ten times the speed it should. But you wouldn't have two or three hours to yourself, not in a place like this. So this lad did something else. And remember, one stud is all you need — the other three are multiple spares.'

Thane sighed. 'Dan, for — '

'All right.' Laurence grinned. 'Here it is, a three-minute job. Thirty seconds to get the glass panel off, two minutes to remove one of the four clock movements and substitute a new one, thirty seconds to get the glass panel back in place. Here's the new one' — he tapped the bottom of the four sections in the panel — 'and it's a wee beauty. Completes its operation in five minutes, whatever the outer dial is set to register. The stud is on an independent clockwork relay. The safe seems closed, but in five minutes you've got the jackpot.'

'Provided the combination lock isn't set, or you know the lock's code,' qualified Thane almost bitterly. 'Any ideas on where this gimmick could come from?'

'Switzerland according to the cover,' said Laurence cynically. 'It's identical with the rest. But as for what's inside — well, it isn't Swiss and it wasn't made in this country.' He raised one bushy eyebrow. 'Do I have to spell it out in front of the peasants?'

Thane shook his head. 'No. And thanks, Dan.'

'As you said, the man who did this would also need to know the combination,' ruminated Laurence. 'And he'd need to have opportunity to be in here during the day.'

'The man — or woman,' said Moss bleakly.

'Or woman,' agreed Laurence. 'That's your worry, Colin, not mine. We'll take this wee toy back to Headquarters and play wi' it for a spell. But we'll leave the casing, and the other clocks are workin', so there's no need to mention it to the Hydrostat people unless you feel inclined. Oh — ' he snapped his fingers in recollection. 'We had a go at Carter's house like you asked. His prints are the only ones on his car. We found his own, his wife's and David Stanley's in the house an' another set we think are the housekeeper's. We'll check her out in the morning.'

Clockwork gadgets, classified plans which could have been inspected at leisure any time after working hours — Thane thought briefly and ruefully of Commander Allowes. The Admiralty man was going to be very unhappy.

Five people had known the combination lock's sequence. One was dead — which left Lynne Carter and David Stanley, Peter Hayston and Jane Maulden. Ian Shaw was another character to be kept on file. Even Kelly, the P.R. man, might require checking. A new thought struck him.

'Where did they stow the stuff from this box?'

MacLeod answered. 'It's down in the cashier's safe for the night, sir.' He fidgeted. 'Eh . . . will you need me any more now?'

Thane yawned, knowing how he felt. 'No, off you go, Mac.' As the sergeant escaped from the room he turned to Moss. 'Phil, find a telephone and give Division a call — let's hope this rain is keeping our neds indoors.'

'There's a line plugged through to the secretary's office,' volunteered Laurence. 'That's the one we've been using.'

'Fine.' Thane stretched himself, sighed, and began heading for the door. 'I'll take a look at the cashier's office, just to feel happier. Phil, I'll meet you down at the car.'

Moss nodded and finished unwrapping a bismuth tablet. He'd make the call. But, like the others, he knew the weather could be a stronger crime deterrent than any police force

— and anyway, there would have to be king-sized trouble before he intended to do more than tell the Millside duty team to keep things warm till morning.

* * *

The cashier's office was on the ground floor, the last door on the left along a length of stone-floored corridor. The corridor lights were still burning, and Colin Thane ambled along in no hurry.

He arrived at the glass door with the word 'Cashier' in bold black lettering, reached for the handle, then froze for an instant. The room beyond was in darkness, but either his imagination was playing a trick or a brief scuffling noise had come from inside. The corridor's light meant that to anyone in there he was already a silhouette through the glass — he listened again, but heard nothing.

Slowly, carefully, Thane eased the handle then threw the door open. He took a step forward, peered into the deep shadows of the room, and reached for the light switch on the wall. As his fingers touched it, one of the shadows suddenly moved.

The camera flash-bulb, triggered at a range of little more than six feet, aimed at his eyes, burned into his sight and left a stunning red and white dazzle. He lurched forward, groping blindly. A figure smashed against him hard and fast, knocking him back against the wall and tearing free from his flailing arms. He registered a vague shape running fast along the corridor, tried to follow, and promptly crashed into the door-frame. Cursing, his eyes still half-blinded, Thane set off in clumsy pursuit.

At the corridor's end he hesitated. One way led towards the machine shops, the other to a stores section. He took the latter, found a door lying open, and plunged out into the dark and rain of the factory's central courtyard. A shout rang out from the direction of the street gateway, followed by a harsh flash of light and a second, angrier bellow.

When he reached the gate the uniformed man on guard was swearing bitterly and rubbing hard at his eyes.

'Hey — ' the man started towards him, then gave a groan as he recognised Thane's tall figure. 'He got out, sir — blinded me near enough with some damned light.'

'Did you get a look at him first?'

'No, just a shape. I think — ' the man stopped as Thane brushed past him.

The duty car was parked outside, but it was empty. Thane looked up and down the deserted, rain-soaked street, gave up, and turned back into the factory yard as other figures hurried from the building. Moss came first, followed by their driver.

'We'd a visitor,' he told Moss briefly, then glared at the driver. 'Where the hell were you?'

The man gulped. 'Sorry, sir. I'd just nipped in for — '

Thane didn't wait for an explanation. 'Let's see what he got, Phil.'

The two Millside men hurried through the building and into the cashier's room. Thane switched on the light and took a deep breath of relief. The window blinds had been drawn and ledgers and record files, removed from the safe to make way for its temporary contents, were piled on a table and on part of the floor. But the safe itself, set against an inner wall, was closed — and stayed that way when Moss tried an experimental tug on its handle.

'In here, practically under our feet!' Thane's face was hard and angry. 'He's got nerve, I'll give him that much.'

'He got in, he got out — ' Moss wiped a dribble of rain from his face. 'But why?'

Thane shrugged and crossed to the safe. It was an old model, more a fireproof cabinet than anything else. But the lock hadn't been

110

tampered with — which meant either they'd been lucky or something else had been the camera's target. Something else? That pretty well came down to the company ledgers, and where was the sense in it?

The camera . . .

'Phil, he used two photo-flash bulbs, one here, one when he got past the man at the gate.'

'And maybe he was careless?' Moss nodded.

They found what they wanted just inside the door leading to the courtyard, a small and blackened camera flash bulb with a screw-cap metal base. Moss lifted it carefully then glanced sideways at his companion as they read the 'Made in Canada' legend stamped on the metal.

'Ian Shaw,' said Thane softly.

'There's such a thing as imports,' reminded Moss carefully. 'A lot of camera stuff comes from over there.' But it was worth checking on, that much he had to agree.

★　★　★

The driver whisked them out to Shaw's motel in record time and a hurt silence. They stopped at the entrance to the site, a grassy open space where about twenty small chalets were spaced at regular intervals round a slightly larger building which served as the manager's quarters.

''Evening, sir.' D.C. Hamilton, the night team man who'd drawn the watch detail, came towards them as they left the car.

'Any sign of movement from Shaw's place?' demanded Thane.

The man shook his head. 'Nothing since I took over, sir. And the Volkswagen's still here.'

'We'll pay him a visit.' Thane gestured Hamilton to lead the way, thankful that the rain had eased back to a drizzle.

Shaw's chalet was the fourth on the left, one of the few in which a light was burning. Music came softly from a radio as they reached the door.

Thane pressed the bell. A moment later the radio clicked off, they heard a creak of springs, the sound of someone moving around, then the door opened a cautious few inches.

'Yes?' Ian Shaw looked round the narrow gap, his red hair tousled, his long-jawed face frowning a little.

'Police,' said Thane briefly, showing his warrant card.

'Oh.' Shaw hesitated, saw the others and shrugged. 'Well — better come in.'

'Thanks.' Thane led the way, and Shaw's

112

keen inspection changed to recognition as they entered the lighted room.

'Hey, you were at the Hydrostat plant this afternoon, weren't you?'

'And now I'm here.' Thane looked around the simply furnished room. The rumpled top cover of the narrow bed, an opened magazine and a small transistor set lying beside it, showed how Shaw had been relaxing. The young engineer wore a jersey and slacks, and his feet were bare. 'Been out tonight, Mr Shaw?'

'Early on, but — '

'Since then?' queried Thane briefly. 'In the last hour or so, for instance?'

'Not me.' Shaw was almost too positive. 'Why?'

'We're interested. Mind if we look around?'

He shrugged. 'Be my guest.'

Phil Moss and Hamilton set to work. In a few brief minutes, while Shaw watched, the room had been combed from end to end. A small kitchen and an even smaller bathroom were the only other apartments, and by the time they were finished they could have made an inventory of the motel chalet's contents down to the last tin of beans.

'Just these,' reported Moss. He held up a damp raincoat and a pair of shoes which had soles caked with a mixture of mud and ash.

'Like I told you, I was out earlier,' declared Shaw uneasily. 'What's going on?'

Thane warmed his back in the glow from a small electric radiator. 'Call it making inquiries, Mr Shaw. Do you own a camera?'

'No.' The young engineer's jaw firmed and he started forward. 'Now listen — '

Phil Moss's hand landed on Shaw's shoulder with surprising strength. 'You listen, lad,' he advised acidly. 'And take it easy.'

Shaw glared around him for a moment then went back to the bed and sat on its edge. 'Well?'

'That's better,' said Thane briskly. 'Now let's save some time. Why did you come back from Canada?'

'An aunt died and left me some money and a houseful of furniture,' said Shaw briefly. 'I'm her only relative and there were things to settle.'

'Lawyers can do it,' reminded Moss.

'But I wanted a trip home. Any objections?'

'A twenty-one day excursion trip,' reminded Thane. 'Then you cancel your return flight and take a job.'

'I decided to stay on for a spell,' shrugged Shaw. 'What's the crime? Or — wait a minute!' He gave a slow grin of cynical understanding. 'I'm working for Hydrostat Drives, they're on defence contract projects

114

— this is some kind of a security once-over, right?'

'Right and wrong,' Thane told him. 'There also happens to be a murder, Mr Shaw. The story I got from the works manager is that Carter interviewed you for this job on Friday. But according to someone else this 'interview' sounded more like good-going battle.'

Shaw's broad mouth twisted ruefully. 'Dark hair, nice legs and a look that would freeze you — I know who you mean.' He shrugged. 'Well, she heard an argument all right. But you don't murder a character just because he won't offer you enough money.'

'You're saying that's what it was about?'

'Uh-huh.' Shaw relaxed back on his elbows. 'The difference between what we thought I was worth per week. I wasn't desperate for the job unless the pay was right.'

Thane's face registered brief disbelief, but he moved on. 'If that's what happened, then you won't mind telling me where you were yesterday afternoon.'

'I didn't do much.'

'We're still interested.'

Shaw shrugged. 'I drove through to Edinburgh, had a meal, and went down to have a look at the Forth Road Bridge.'

'Sight-seeing?' Moss raised a doubtful eyebrow.

Shaw regarded him with something approaching disdain. 'I happen to be an engineer, remember? They were just starting to build the bridge when I left for Canada, and it happens to be the biggest in Europe. So I went sight-seeing, then drove back here and didn't budge.'

'Any way of proving you made this trip?' queried Thane.

'Easy enough.' Shaw's voice gathered confidence. 'I spoke to one of the bridge maintenance men — talked to him for quite a spell. He'll remember me.'

'Let's hope he does,' said Thane quietly. 'Sometime tomorrow we'll have a man round asking for your fingerprints, Mr Shaw.'

'For you — or for the job?'

'I don't know yet.' Thane nodded to the others and they turned to go. 'Good night, Mr Shaw.'

Shaw lay back on the bed, reaching for his magazine. ''Bye, then,' he grinned cheerfully. 'Look in any time.'

★   ★   ★

There was plenty of work to organise when they got back to Millside, inquiries which could be under way during the night. The end result was that it was past midnight before

116

one of the divisional patrol cars took Thane home and deposited him at his front gate.

The porch light was still burning. He smiled at the sight, waved his thanks as the car pulled away, then walked up the path towards the little bungalow. The wet scent of the garden's rose bushes hung heavy in the air as he found his key and turned it in the lock.

A tan-and-white tornado of young boxer dog burst from the far end of the hallway as he entered. He struggled past Clyde's greeting, closed the door, almost tripped over the bounding dog, and heard a soft chuckle of laughter.

Mary Thane was dark-haired, with a smooth, fresh complexion and a figure which made nonsense of the fact that she had two children of school age.

She came towards him, a smile of welcome on her lips. 'I'd almost given you up for lost,' she declared.

'I'd almost given myself up,' confessed Thane. He fended off the dog, gave her a brief peck of a kiss, then held her for a moment or so longer than usual.

Mary knew the signs. 'Tired?'

'Uh-huh.'

'Any luck with Phil's problem?'

He'd practically forgotten the Emma

Robertson business. 'No, not much. I doubt if she'd listen anyway.'

'We'll think of something.' She winked at him. 'Supper's on the tray and the kettle's been boiled. Ready?'

'Any time,' he agreed.

Thane wandered into the front room, the dog still fussing round his heels. There were toys scattered on his usual armchair and he cleared them slowly, grinning as he came across young Tommy's current favourite, a bright red plastic ray-gun. Handy if it was real, instead of just a glorified water pistol. He hefted it, sighted along the barrel, and imagined several possible candidates for extermination. Like Superintendent Donfoot, for instance — or Splits Clark. He pressed the trigger, and a jet of water spurted out to drench across the carpet.

He was on hands and knees, mopping up with a handkerchief, when Mary appeared with the supper tray. She shook her head at the sight.

'Never play with a loaded gun,' she said solemnly.

Thane waited till she'd put the tray down, then swung the pistol in her direction.

'Try it, Colin Thane,' she dared. 'Just try it and see what happens.'

He saw the laughter in her eyes, grinned

back, and knew that here, at any rate, he could forget the world outside.

★ ★ ★

Bright morning sunlight was pouring into their bedroom when Thane wakened. It was a little after seven-thirty, Mary was already moving around downstairs, and he fought off the temptation to laze where he was. By the time he'd washed and shaved, Tommy and Kate were wandering around in their pyjamas and he had to sort out a row about who was next in line for the bathroom. He finished dressing and went downstairs, to find the dog already out for its morning stroll, the table set for breakfast, and bacon sizzling in a pan.

'Morning,' greeted Mary.

He kissed her lightly, inspected her rose-pink housecoat, and shook his head. 'Either that thing's shrinking or you're getting fat.'

'Shrinking,' she said complacently. 'And I need a new one.'

The telephone rang. He went through to the hall and lifted the receiver.

'Thane.'

'Air traffic control, Abbotsinch,' said a bright voice at the other end of the line. 'I've been told to advise you of a British European

119

Airways charter flight coming in from Switzerland.'

'For Hydrostat Drives?'

'That's the one,' agreed the airport official. 'She's a Bristol freighter, on direct flight from Basle. Due for touch-down here in about an hour. Okay?'

Thane thanked the man, hung up, then lifted the receiver again and dialled the Millside Division number. When he got through he gave the switchboard a message to be passed on to Phil Moss, arranged for a car to collect him, and spoke briefly to the duty inspector on the uniformed branch. He hung up again, heard the dog scratching at the front door, let him in, then went through and joined the others for breakfast.

Tommy kept an eye on the window. Halfway through the last slice of toast he gulped, almost choked himself and declared, 'Hey, look!'

A long, sleek Mercedes two-seater, a slash of scarlet colour, had pulled in at the kerb. The small, rotund figure in the driver's seat beamed around him. The twin horns gave a blast of sound.

Commander Allowes had arrived in style.

Thane gulped the last of his coffee, kissed wife and children in swift rotation, then grabbed his hat and left.

Allowes had the passenger door open by the time Thane reached the pavement's edge. He greeted him cheerfully. 'Like a lift? I'm heading out to the airport.'

'Well — '

'Your own car?' Allowes waved a podgy hand. 'I telephoned Millside. They know I'm collecting you.'

Thane scrambled aboard. As he settled into the open cockpit Allowes flicked the car into gear, pressed the accelerator, and they jerked away.

'Oops.' Allowes slowed a little as they reached a corner, but still took it in a scream of tyre rubber. 'My own car's in dock for repairs. Borrowed this from my secretary.'

Thane winced as the Mercedes surged forward, climbing through the revs. 'Who is she — an admiral's daughter?'

'Well, yes, among other things.' Allowes grated the next gear change and almost mounted the kerb. 'Now, what's this I heard about some nonsense with Carter's safe?'

Thane told him of the time-lock substitution and the rest while the car travelled on in the same nerve-wracking fashion.

'Interesting,' mused Allowes. 'I've only one little crumb I can offer in return.' The round face was blandly innocent. 'It doesn't help my little problem, but Carter's widow and David

Stanley can make themselves very well off once they get Carter's affairs settled up. All they'll have to do is sign a piece of paper — and make about a hundred thousand pounds apiece.'

'How?' Thane was too amazed to bother about a jaywalking pedestrian who'd just had to dive for safety.

'A take-over bid. The D.R. Engineering group are trying hard to swing the deal.'

Thane's mouth tightened. When one of the biggest engineering organisations in Britain went shopping for a company they could afford to make the terms generous. A possible two-way split, plus the chance to dispose of an unwanted husband — the Admiralty man's 'crumb' left plenty to think about.

★　★　★

They reached the airport terminal building in time to be told that the charter plane was already on its approach run.

'She's being taken straight over to the cargo area,' advised a pipe-smoking B.E.A. controller who'd been waiting their arrival. 'We've a special request from the Hydrostat company to bring her in where she can be unloaded without an audience.'

A few brief directions, and they headed the

car on a threading route round the narrow service roads which flanked the Abbotsinch runways. Halfway to their destination, there was a sudden roar overhead and a momentary shadow passed across the car as the big Bristol freighter's silver shape swept low above them, coming in to land. She touched down smoothly and began taxi-ing.

When the Mercedes purred into the cargo area the freight plane was already there, her engines silent, the big unloading door in her nose swinging open. Lynne Carter's black Alfa and a couple of other cars were parked nearby beside a transporter truck, and there were several familiar faces among the waiting cluster of people.

'The widow Carter looks well in black,' murmured Allowes, letting his car coast to a halt beside the others.

Thane nodded. Lynne Carter wasn't in full mourning, but the black tailored suit she wore set off her long blonde hair to perfection. She stood with David Stanley, a little way apart from the main group of about a dozen who were watching the aircraft's unloading ramps being run out. A few were airport and customs staff, but the majority were Hydrostat employees. One of them turned, saw Thane leaving the car, and gave a brief, cynical wave.

'A friend?' queried Allowes, joining him.

'Ian Shaw,' said Thane dryly as they began heading across the tarmac.

'Ah, your young man from Canada!' Allowes looked again with keener interest. 'There's a girl there, too — on the far side.'

Thane had a brief glimpse of Jane Maulden, a sheaf of papers in her hands, her attention occupied by what one of the airport officials was saying, then Allowes gave him a nudge and spoke in a louder voice.

'Hello there, David — '

'Commander — good to see you!' David Stanley's broad face crinkled in a friendly welcome. The expression faded a little as he turned towards Thane. 'I'd a feeling you'd show up, Chief Inspector.'

Thane nodded. 'You'll have to get used to me being around for a spell.' He glanced towards the blonde. 'Everything all right, Mrs Carter?'

'Yes.' She awarded him a faint smile. 'Everyone's being very kind.'

'With reason,' said Allowes sympathetically. 'And if my department can help — ' he let the offer hang, unfinished.

'It's a rough time,' growled Stanley protectively. 'I brought Lynne out this morning to try and take her mind off it for a spell. And I'm wanting her to come north

124

with us tonight — for one thing, it would keep her clear of those blasted reporters buzzing around.'

'It sounds a good idea,' agreed Allowes.

'Commander — ' Lynne Carter laid a gloved hand on his arm. 'Do you think — well, could Bill's death have been because of the drawings in the safe?'

Allowes puffed his cheeks expressively. 'Ask the Chief Inspector,' he suggested. 'You know my job — I just take care of the paperwork.'

'What about it, Thane?' demanded Stanley. 'I'd like to know, too. And there's a buzz around the plant that something happened in the office block last night. Is it true?'

'We found a prowler,' said Thane briefly, mentally cursing whoever had let that little item slip out. 'The main gate was open for a spell and somebody sneaked in then was chased off again.' They were both watching him, waiting for the rest of his answer. He shrugged. 'I'm sorry, Mrs Carter, all I can say about the rest is we're doing several things — what happens next depends on the results.'

Stanley gave an expressive grunt and turned away — but Thane could have sworn that something close to relief passed between him and the tight-lipped woman by his side.

Over at the freight plane a fresh bustle of activity was under way. A car appeared at the opened nose door, its wheels were guided on to the ramp tracks, and it rolled slowly down to the tarmac. The man who'd been at the wheel jumped out and waved.

'There's our baby,' said Stanley, with a brief, confident grin. 'This time tomorrow she'll be making a lot of people sit up and take notice.'

To Thane, the car out on the tarmac seemed a perfectly ordinary medium-sized family saloon, the colour grey, the body riding perhaps a little high on its springs.

Stanley appeared to read his thoughts. 'Sure, it looks ordinary enough. Most ghost cars do — that's the trade tag for experimental jobs. What we did was buy a low-mileage used car, scrap every working part, and build our own machinery inside the shell.'

'Machinery plenty of people would like to see,' said Commander Allowes thoughtfully.

'But there'll be no show today,' declared Stanley. 'We've too much to do. Lynne, mind if I leave you for a spell?'

She shook her head. 'I can wait in my car.'

'Fine. I'll collect Jane Maulden and get the customs formalities sorted out.' He grimaced towards Thane. 'By the time we have that done and gather up what's waiting at the plant there'll be quite a convoy heading north

— and it's going to be a long day's drive.'

'I'll walk over with you, Mrs Carter,' volunteered Allowes. She smiled down at the roly-poly security man, and they began walking back towards the waiting Alfa.

'Now then' — Stanley raised his voice — 'Jane!' The dark-haired secretary looked round at his shout and headed towards him.

'Taking her with the test team?' queried Thane.

'Jane?' Stanley nodded. 'She'll have plenty to do.'

'Then I'd better have a word with her now,' Thane told him. 'I think she can help us.'

David Stanley ran an impatient hand through his hair. 'Well, keep it short, will you?' He sighed as the girl reached them. 'Jane, the police want to talk to you again — make it short as you can.'

She flushed as he went striding off towards the aircraft. Most of the others were heading in the same direction, and the transporter truck had begun rolling forward to collect its load.

'I'll keep it brief,' Thane assured her.

'Good.' The girl frowned down at the papers in her hands. 'I've got the clearance documents to attend to and a lot more besides.'

A fully-laden Viscount turbo-prop took off

from the main runway, the blast of sound from its four engines drowning Thane's reply. He grimaced, waited until the plane began to climb and the noise died, and tried again. 'Jane, you were one of the few people who always knew the code for the main safe's combination lock. I want to know how often Carter changed that code.'

She frowned, puzzled. 'About once a fortnight, but — '

'When was the combination last changed?'

'On Friday afternoon.'

'Just after you overheard this quarrel between Shaw and Mr Carter?'

Jane Maulden pursed her lips and nodded.

'Had it been a fortnight since the previous change?'

'No, less than a week.' The girl was unhappy, knowing what meaning could be read into her words. 'Mr Thane, I'm not saying that this man Shaw — '

'Neither am I.' Thane looked at her without expression. 'Jane, last night I checked through the list of items found in Carter's office. Didn't he keep any kind of a desk diary?'

'Yes — ' she appeared genuinely surprised. 'But I thought you had it, the police I mean. I can't find it anywhere!'

Another plane was coming in to land. He watched it touch down, then nodded. 'That's all I wanted to ask. You'd better get over before your boss starts worrying.'

'I suppose so.' She looked at him, than at the papers in her hands, nodded, and walked slowly away.

Thane took out his cigarettes, put one in his mouth, then remembered the airport's 'No Smoking' regulations and slipped it into his top pocket. What he needed to do was to get back to Millside, get back to a desk, a telephone, and a chance to check and assemble the collection of fragments he'd accumulated.

'All alone and nothing to do, Chief Inspector?'

He turned at the voice. Ian Shaw stood a few feet away, thumbs hitched into the waistband of his denim overalls, another, older man by his side. The young Scots-Canadian grinned with a cheerful insolence. 'Your boys were out first thing this morning for those fingerprint samples. Anything else you need?'

Thane grunted. 'When there is, we'll let you know.'

A strange expression wisped across Shaw's face. He crossed towards Thane on his own, his voice dropping to a quiet murmur. 'Try somewhere else, Thane. You're fishing the wrong pool, no matter what that girl may think.' Then he brightened and beckoned his companion over. 'Danny, come and meet the Chief Inspector.'

The older man came over, moving with a heavy limp. 'Danny Benson,' he introduced himself in a heavy brogue. 'I've seen you around, Mr Thane.'

The Hydrostat plant's head foreman was bald and stocky, with a wrinkled weather-beaten face and dark, deep-set eyes. 'There's a lot o' us hopin' you'll get the devil who killed Mr Carter,' he said earnestly. 'He was pretty good as bosses go.'

'Been with him long?' queried Thane.

Benson shook his head. 'Cars are my game, Mr Thane — were, anyway, till I got this.' He tapped his right leg significantly. 'I was on prototype crew wi' most o' the big outfits — B.M.C., Ford, Jaguar an' the rest. Travelled most places wi' them, too. Then I had to pack it in an' go back to bein' an engineer. They hadn't even thought o' this hydrostatic transmission business when I got the job.'

'And now he's as happy as a pig in a mudbath,' said Shaw easily. 'Mind if I go on over, Danny?'

Benson sighed as the younger man went off. 'A smart lad,' he muttered half to himself. 'Just a wee bit too smart at times, but he'll

130

learn.' The man brightened. 'First time you've seen a ghost car, Mr Thane?'

'I never even thought of them before,' admitted Thane.

'Aye, few do,' chuckled Benson. 'But it's a life that gets you around. I smashed this leg o' mine in East Africa, tropical-testin' a wee sports car. It was a stinker — they scrapped the whole idea. Plenty end up that way.'

'Even with the big firms?'

'Especially wi' the big firms,' emphasised Benson. 'They're the only folk who can go the limit — it costs a hell o' a lot o' money to get one off the drawin' board, then the prototypes maybe knock up a quarter million miles before anyone even admits they ruddy well exist.' He chuckled again. 'Aye, an' there's one due out next year, a saloon, that did a lot more mileage than that before we got the last o' the bugs out o' her.'

'Next year?' Thane frowned. 'That means you were working on it — '

'Four years ago,' nodded Benson, a touch of nostalgia in his voice. 'Finland for cold-weather tests, Nevada for long-distance roadwork, then up in the Highlands here for the final sessions. It's a long time from prototype before the things start beltin' off the production line.'

'They keep pretty quiet about them, then,'

murmured Thane.

'They have to. If one outfit knew what the other was playin' wi' — ' Benson drew a finger significantly across his throat — 'that's it. The world's a hard, cold place. So we bring out the old disguise-box — dirty up the body. A polished car stands out like a ruddy signal. Or there's a faked bodyline, wi' maybe a false curve or two made up o' brown paper or chicken wire, sprayed over wi' paint. No badges, no chrome, no name-plates — unless they're somebody else's.'

Thane grinned. 'What happens if you're caught?'

'We make dam' sure we're not.' Benson's eyes crinkled at a memory. 'I was wi' one job once, in France, an' we were usin' badges pretendin' to be — well, another mob. An' who do we bump into but their outfit, an' they're carryin' our firm's badges. What would you do, eh?'

A squeal of brakes saved Thane from having to answer. The new arrival, a big old-model station wagon, had pulled to a stop a few yards away. Bart Kelly tumbled out of the driver's seat and hurried over, carrying a briefcase.

'How long since that damned plane touched down?'

'Ten minutes, not much more,' Thane told him.

The grey-haired public relations man swore. As much in need of a shave as ever, he was dressed for the outdoors in an old leather jacket, heavy wool shirt and whipcord slacks. 'First I oversleep because I didn't get to bed till three this morning, then that heap I call a car wouldn't start — '

'At a late party last night?' queried Thane.

'Working,' corrected Kelly indignantly. 'Two clients with their own ideas on how to run an advertising campaign. As my old mother always said, too many cooks spoil the broth — and the way they wanted things, it looked more like spaghetti.' He sighed. 'Thank heaven this isn't a picture job.'

Thane kept his voice casual. 'You do your own picture stuff as well?'

Kelly shook his head. 'Not me — wouldn't know how. I use agency men, or some newspaper photoman with a day off and a yen for extra cash.' He glared towards Benson. 'Danny, come on over. You can show me what's happening.'

Benson grinned, gave a quick murmur of farewell, and followed the agitated Kelly across the tarmac.

After a moment, Thane turned on his heel and walked back towards the parked

Mercedes. He had climbed into the passenger seat and was settled before he noticed the small white envelope propped against the central gear lever.

Puzzled, he opened it, and something small and paper-like fluttered out on to his lap.

When Commander Allowes ambled over a minute later, he found his passenger smoking a cigarette in defiance of all regulations and still staring at his find.

'What's wrong?' demanded Allowes.

'We've a joker in the pack,' grated Thane.

The photograph was small in size, but it showed Colin Thane's face in a startled, open-mouthed close-up.

And its subject didn't need to study the background detail to know where it had been taken.

The prowler at the Hydrostat cashier's office had, among other things, a definite sense of humour!

5

It was close on 11 a.m. and Phil Moss sat at a small table against one wall in Thane's office, typing doggedly on an old-style portable. Headquarters wanted a new report on the Carter case, and Detective Superintendent Donfoot's message had said it was to be ready by noon.

Using a two finger and thumb technique all his own, Moss thumped the typewriter's space bar with a determined violence as each word took shape. He'd already roughed out the first draft and was starting on the final version. He slipped the first page from the machine, read it through, and belched with a luxuriant resonance. On the floor above, two clerks in the quiet Summons Office broke off working for a moment and shook their heads in silent admiration.

The report's second page was taking shape when the room door opened and Thane strode in.

'Where's the picture?' Moss slid round in his chair, a grin slanting across his face. 'If it's good, put me down for a dozen copies — '

'Welcome to comedy hour.' Thane snorted,

shoved his hat on the peg behind the door, and briefly regretted the 'phone call he'd made to Millside from the airport. He crossed the room to the divisional wall-map, and glanced briefly at the dozen or so fresh pin-heads which had sprouted overnight. They were colour-coded, identifying a handful of burglaries, roughly the same number of assaults and a double razor-slashing ... a challenge match between a couple of neds, according to the first reports.

'I said where's your picture,' persisted Moss.

'At Headquarters, being mounted and framed,' retorted Thane with heavy sarcasm. He perched on the edge of his desk, one leg swinging, and asked, 'Got Donfoot's report finished yet?'

Moss shook his head. 'No, but it won't be long. I've worked out a nicely confusing way of saying that we're not really chasing our own tails in ever-decreasing circles.' He grimaced. 'I just hope it comes true.'

'I know what you mean,' admitted Thane ruefully. 'Anything fresh?'

'Nothing that's likely to give you happy thoughts.' Moss abandoned the typewriter. 'Colin, it comes down to a nice, round zero. Almost, anyway. Take that works manager Hayston and this foreman Benson, the other keyholder. Their stories check out — Hayston spent all of Sunday with friends in the country. Benson was on a bus outing, with thirty ruddy members of a social club as witnesses.'

Thane shrugged. 'What matters is whether either of them has allowed his keys to be copied — and they're not going to come in and admit it.'

The whole question of the Hydrostat keys worried him. Carter's keys had been taken or were at least missing — but why? No sign of a break-in at the plant seemed to mean either that Carter had admitted somebody he knew or that the intruder had keys. That somebody could have taken the keys to lock up as he left — or in an attempt to hide the fact that he possessed a set of his own.

'Then there's the Maulden girl,' mused Moss. 'She's another who was out of town, through in Edinburgh.'

'Pleasure trip?' Thane raised an eyebrow.

'Visiting her father,' corrected Moss. 'He's in a home for incurables. The ward sister says she arrived in the afternoon and stayed till late evening — she does the same thing every Sunday.'

'Which pretty well rules her out.' Thane leaned back across the desk, flicked the intercom switch, and told the duty orderly to find some tea. He frowned as he released the switch. 'How about Shaw?'

'Slightly better.' Moss rifled through the papers at his side. 'Toronto cabled us — here it is.' He waved the buff form briefly. 'His firm out there have him on their medical files as blood group B, which ties in with the nasal samples.'

The news was only in the signpost category. Blood group evidence was mainly important as an innocence factor, the kind that could prove positively that a specimen hadn't come from a particular individual. On guilt, all it could say was that blood found was identical in group to a possible source.

Still, Shaw being group B kept him in the running . . . 'I picked up a crumb at Headquarters, Phil. The fingerprint squad have identified his prints in Carter's office.'

'And he can say they got there on Friday, when he had that interview,' grunted Moss. 'Any luck at the house?'

'The last set of prints belonged to the housekeeper.' Thane chewed a corner of one thumbnail as the door opened. The young police cadet who padded in laid two steaming mugs of tea on the desk, glanced at Thane, then went out silently as he'd come.

'What's got into him?' queried Thane.

'Take a look in the mirror,' suggested Moss

dryly. 'You left your happy face at home this morning.'

Thane sipped his tea, frowned, and gave the dark brown liquid a stir with a pencil. 'I'd be happier if I could make sense out of last night's camera business,' he confessed.

'Don't they use cameras in the P.R. business?'

'He says he hires from outside — anyway, he couldn't have planted that snapshot in the car.' Thane tried the tea again and found it better. 'Being in public relations doesn't make him an enemy of humanity, and he's got an alibi for last night.'

'How about for Sunday?' queried Moss. 'We don't know — and I've got young Beech outside doing dam' all for a living. I could put him to work.'

The idea was appealing, but Thane had something else on his mind. 'Let me see what we've got on the Hydrostat background.'

Wordlessly, Moss handed over two stapled sheets of close-typed paper. Thane walked round to his chair, sank down, and skimmed through the breakdown. Hydrostat Drives had no apparent financial worries, just the usual working overdraft arrangement with their bankers, one their assets could cover several times over. The first approach in D.R. Engineering's take-over bid had been six

139

months back and had been politely rejected. The second attempt, with the ante considerably upped, had been made within the last month — and so far there had been no reply.

'What about Carter's lawyer?'

Moss swallowed another mouthful of tea before replying. 'Knows nothing.' He wiped his mouth with the back of one thin hand. 'He's just the man who takes care of formalities. They've a chartered accountant in the same category — comes along to audit, gets the odd phone call and sends a bill in once a year. And while we're at it, Mrs Carter hasn't done anything yet about having her car serviced — if it needs it.'

Thane nodded gloomily, cursing the fact that his whole mad caravan of suspects were now happily driving north. Somehow, somewhere, there had to be reason behind the tangle. The hard fact of Carter's murder, the half-formed pattern of espionage — did they have to be linked, yet could they possibly be separate? How many factors was he dealing with, how many issues with a common boiling point?

'And what's our sweet-talking Commander Allowes doing about it all?' demanded Moss, as if mind-reading. 'For somebody who should be out spy-catching he's being pretty quiet.'

'You know these security mobs, Phil. Always happy to let some other outfit do their legwork.' Allowes had given him a lift back to Headquarters, recalled Thane ruefully. The entire conversation had been about the weather. A brief knock on the door stopped him telling about it, and D.C. Beech poked his head into the room.

'Sir — '

'We were talking about you, laddie,' said Moss briskly. 'A wee job you could maybe do.'

Beech was unimpressed. 'I've a man outside wanting to see you, sir,' he told Thane. 'Eh . . . I've tried to chase him, but he's determined.'

'What name?' queried Thane.

'A Mr Clark,' said Beech, his face slightly puzzled. 'I've seen him somewhere but — '

'You've seen him,' agreed Thane with an ominous glance towards Moss. 'Probably in the dock. Look him up in the files and you'll improve your education.'

'He says it's private and personal, sir.' Beech looked more worried than before. 'What will I do with him?'

'I'll see him,' decided Thane. As Beech nodded and went out, he noticed Phil Moss edging towards the open door. 'And don't try to sneak off, Phil. This is your pigeon.'

His second-in-command gave a wry shrug and stayed where he was. In a matter of moments Beech reappeared and beckoned the man behind him to enter.

'Clark, sir.'

'Right.' Thane waved their visitor towards the chair on the other side of the desk. 'Sit down, Splits.'

'Thanks.' Arthur Robert 'Splits' Clark moved stiffly across the room, glared briefly in Moss's direction, and took the offered chair.

Splits Clark was, in appearance at any rate, a cut or two above the usual ned. A heavily-jowelled yet still vaguely handsome man in his mid-fifties, only a little grey around the temples, he had a small, neatly trimmed moustache and when his lips parted a flash of gold filling showed in a front tooth. A white shirt, quiet tie and dark business suit went with well-polished shoes, a chunky gold watch and an equally chunky gold signet ring — the counterfeiter always made a habit of looking his best when it came to business, appearing in the dock, or penetrating police stations.

'That's all, Beech.' Colin Thane waited until the youngster had gone out and the door was closed. 'Well now, Splits, I haven't seen you for quite a spell — '

142

'I'd prefer Mr Clark, Chief Inspector,' said the man with a peevish dignity. 'That is, if you don't mind.'

Thane regarded him with a new interest for a moment, then nodded. 'All right, Mister Clark — and of course, you know Inspector Moss.'

'He's why I'm here, and you know it.' Clark sat erect and watchful on the edge of the chair. 'I'm a member of the public, and I'm making a complaint.'

'I see.' Thane's fingers strayed to the pencil on his desk and he toyed with it gently. 'Well, suppose you tell me.'

Clark took a deep breath. 'You know the law. When a man's served prison time and comes out the thing's finished, done with — '

'Tholed his assize is the phrase,' murmured Thane. 'Go on.'

'The law also says that any deliberate spreading around of the fact that he's been inside, spreading it around in a dirty, malicious way to ruin his private life — '

'If you're talking about me, Clark — ' Moss took a step forward, but was waved to a halt by his friend.

'To ruin his private life?' Thane's face hardened a little. He'd expected it, but hearing Clark, watching the man, he realised afresh just how quickly the counterfeiter

143

would cause trouble given the chance — cause trouble and relish the prospect. 'I'd hate to think you were suggesting anyone in this division was involved.'

'Would you?' Clark sneered at the idea. 'Look, Chief Inspector, you know dam' well what I'm talking about. There's no crime in a man deciding to get married, even if the woman happens to have a ruddy cop as a lodger.'

'So you want me to keep Inspector Moss off your back?' A dangerous edge honed its way into Thane's voice. 'All right, Splits, now I'm going to tell you something. I know all about Emma Robertson, just as I know that Phil Moss has kept his mouth tight shut about who you are and what you are. Maybe you wash your neck more often than some of the rest, but you're still a ned in my book. I don't like neds. I particularly don't like neds who come into my office and start threatening their way around.'

'I've my rights.' Clark was still aggressive, but more careful. 'I've got a job, I've a right to a clean start.'

'Everybody has their rights,' agreed Thane heavily. 'But it happens Emma Robertson has a nice-looking bank balance. Maybe you find that attractive.'

'Eh?' Clark's face twitched. 'Say that

outside and I'll have a lawyer on your doorstep.'

'I'm sure you would.' Thane gripped the pencil between his fingers. 'Splits, you've got a record that covers more than twenty years — '

'Twenty-three,' murmured Moss.

'Twenty-three — thanks, Phil.' He leaned forward a little. 'I think you're lining up a meal ticket for your old age, Splits, and I don't like it. I've an idea you'd have steered clear of Emma Robertson early on if you'd known she'd a cop as a lodger.'

Clark gave a sullen growl. 'All right, it's twenty-three years. But what about before that? I held down a job for long enough and I could do it again.' His face grew ugly, the gold tooth glinted as his mouth twisted. 'I'm telling you straight, both o' you, this is none of your ruddy business.' He gestured towards Moss. 'I can go along to Headquarters and tell them he's been trying to foul up my private life.'

'Do that, and I'll personally break your ruddy neck,' said Moss heatedly.

'That's maybe an exaggeration,' said Thane softly. 'But life would become very difficult.'

'Cops. Once they've got your number that's it, eh?' Clark showed his disgust.

Thane looked at him, then thumbed

towards the door. 'Out.'

'I'll go to Headquarters an' — '

'Out.' Thane glanced towards Moss. 'Phil, help him on his way.'

'If he touches me — ' Clark leapt from his chair and began backing towards the door. In another moment he had gone, the door banging shut behind him. The two Millside men exchanged a grin.

'Our Mr Clark could be troublesome,' mused Thane. 'I don't think he'll try Headquarters, but you're right, Phil. He's on the make, he's worried, and he hates the thought of letting Emma Robertson off the hook.'

The telephone rang. He scooped up the receiver, listened, and grimaced. 'Donfoot,' he said quickly for Moss's benefit, then told the switchboard operator, 'Put him through, Jean.'

The acting C.I.D. chief's chilly tones came crackling over the wires. 'Purely seeking information, Thane. I'm still waiting on that memo on the Carter affair — and it does happen to be of concern to people of considerable importance.'

'You'll have it by noon, sir,' said Thane evasively.

'How much will it tell me?' demanded Superintendent Donfoot in the same icy

146

manner. 'Thane, I've a feeling that certain of the divisions seem reluctant to let me know what's happening in their areas.'

Thane grinned at the mouthpiece but kept his voice politely neutral. 'Well, things are at an awkward stage as far as the Carter business is concerned, sir.'

'A new way of saying no progress?' Donfoot's sniff was loud and clear. 'All right, Thane. I'll wait for the memo.'

'Yes, sir.' Thane heard the receiver thump down at the other end, swore briefly, and replaced his own.

'Yes, sir, no, sir, three bags full, sir — ' Moss chuckled from his corner.

'Get that ruddy thing finished and stop clowning,' growled Thane. 'When it's done, you'd better take it straight over to Headquarters. Then look in at the Scientific Bureau and see if they've anything to tell us about that photograph.'

Moss grinned, settled down at the type-writer, but turned round after he'd tapped less than a dozen letters. 'Colin — '

'Well?'

'What about Clark — what do we do next?'

Thane sighed. 'If I had my way I'd make a package of the pair of you and dump it straight into the Clyde.' He rubbed a hand along his chin, frowning. 'He's not short of

147

money, judging by the way he's dressed. Maybe Emma Robertson's already given him the odd hand-out — '

'Or maybe he's turning out a few dud notes on the side?'

'Maybe. But I don't want this turned into a vendetta, Phil.' Thane pulled the Carter file towards him and flipped it open. 'Now for Pete's sake, let me get on with this.'

Moss mumbled a reply, saw it ignored, and turned back to the typewriter.

★   ★   ★

At Headquarters, someone else was busy at a typewriter. She was secretary to the Scientific Bureau, she had auburn hair, blue eyes, and legs which defied the low-heeled brogues and black heavy-gauge nylons which were standard issue for uniformed policewomen. She could type roughly three times faster than Moss, and the words flowed automatically as she transcribed from her shorthand notebook.

'Examination of photograph received from Chief Detective Inspector C. Thane, Millside Division.

'Photograph shows no trace of fingerprints and is on commercial grade paper readily available to the public. Tone of print suggests

148

slight degree of over-exposure to counter poor quality negative. Glazing is patchy.

'Camera was probably a 35 mm model with a lens of medium optical quality. It had been set for close-range work, in the eighteen-inch to two-foot category. This is calculated from apparent depth of focus shown, with subject's face and nearer edge of door and surface of wall as triangulation points. Accepting that use was to have been for probable copying work, camera setting was that of a reasonably competent amateur rather than a professional, who would have varied setting and probably used better equipment.

'Flecks present on print point to negative being developed under home darkroom conditions. Scissors used to trim print have minor double notch on upper and lower blades, possible result of having been used to cut single-core electrical wiring or similar.'

She whipped the report from her machine, separated the two carbon copies from the original, and put them aside. The next page of notes in her book left her equally bored. It was hard to become excited over a spectro-scopic analysis of wood dust particles, even if it was going to wrap up a safeblowing case for the Eastern Division.

Phil Moss arrived at the Bureau front office

a few minutes after noon — his own report had already been handed to Donfoot's orderly, after which he'd made a hasty retreat.

The detective sergeant at the Bureau's front desk grinned when he saw him. 'You Millside characters don't stand much chance of winning a beauty contest,' he declared, solemnly clipping the snapshot to one corner of the report and passing it over.

'Anything else for us?' queried Moss.

The sergeant shook his head. 'There's quite a fuss going on over that time-lock we lifted from the Hydrostat safe — Superintendent Laurence has gone off to see some pal of his about it. But that's the lot. Sorry.'

Moss grunted and set off again. His next call was the Regional Crime Squad section, two floors down. They were a mixed-manned outfit from several counties, acting as part clearing-house part action co-ordination for the tangle of local forces operation in the whole western sweep of Scotland.

The duty inspector, a Dunbartonshire man, listened to his query and scratched his head. 'Counterfeit notes?' He took one of the cigarettes Moss offered and struck a match before answering. 'No, I haven't heard of any slush-merchants lately. Who've you got in mind, Phil?'

Moss frowned. 'Fellow named Splits Clark.

I've nothing to go on, except that he looks prosperous.'

'Don't they all?' The Dunbartonshire officer smoked in silence for a moment. 'Look, I'll have a word around and let you know.'

Moss hesitated, his conscience stirring. 'I'm not trying to cook anything against him.'

'But you're curious, and that's what keeps us in business.' The other man grinned. 'How's the health?'

'Not too bad,' said Moss cautiously. There was a faint, gathering pang somewhere in his stomach area, but it was probably hunger. 'I watch my diet.'

'Aye, it pays.' The Dunbartonshire officer nodded as Moss went out, then scribbled briefly on a piece of paper and tossed it into a tray. Up at the University there was a computer being designed which would take over this side of his job before long. Feed it all the hunches, sightings and odd titbits of gossip and it would belt out the conclusion that there was going to be a bank raid in High Street at five past two next Tuesday. At least, that was the idea. He'd believe it when it happened.

★　★　★

Colin Thane was halfway through lunch when Moss found him in the little cafe they often used, situated just around the corner from the Millside Division building. While his second-in-command ordered from the gravy-stained menu, he read through the Headquarters report in complete silence. Spies who went to the trouble of rigging fake time-locks on safes didn't use second-rate cameras or work with commercial grade print paper. Even Commander Allowes would have agreed that the Bureau findings pointed away from that possibility.

He folded the report and put it in his pocket.

'What's been happening?' queried Moss.

'Small stuff.' Thane shoved aside the remains of his apple pie. 'I've teletyped Army records asking for David Stanley's blood group. And I got Mac to take another look around the Hydrostat offices for Carter's desk diary. It's still missing, which could mean somebody thinks we might find the entries too interesting.'

'The girl?'

'I doubt it.' Thane lit a cigarette. 'Then we've got confirmation from Edinburgh C.I.D. that Shaw's story about being through there seems genuine, except that he didn't get there till about five in the evening.'

'Which keeps him in the running,' mused Moss. 'How about Kelly?'

Thane shook his head. 'I chased young Beech out on the job. Kelly's two clients of last night are real enough — they were still sleeping it off when he found them. Sunday's still vague, but it looks like he stayed home working most of the day.'

Hunger gnawing, Moss looked around for some sign of his order coming and gave a groan. The cause had just entered the cafe, bare-headed, a raincoat covering his uniform. Inspector Bradford ran the Inquiry Department, rated as a harmless character, but had only one stock conversation — football, and more specifically, the team he worshipped, Glasgow Rangers.

Bradford saw them, waved, and strode over.

'I've been looking for you two,' he declared.

'If it's a body from the river and relatives are wanted we're too busy to help,' warned Thane. Bradford's floaters, mostly suicides, were a constant thorn.

'A body?' Bradford blinked. 'No, it's a request I've had from Carlisle — one I thought might interest you. It's about Mrs Carter's car.'

'Eh?' Thane's interest sharpened.

'She drives too fast,' said Bradford, settling

uninvited into a vacant chair. 'The Carlisle boys were working a speed trap on the main London — Glasgow road on Sunday, and she belted through doing a clear fifty in a built-up area. They were busy booking somebody else, but they got her number.'

'When did it happen?'

'That's the point,' said Bradford triumphantly. 'Around five o'clock, they say. Yet I gather you sent a service message about the same car to the Welsh forces, asking if it had been seen in their area that afternoon. She strayed a bit, didn't she?'

'She certainly did,' agreed Thane softly. From Carlisle to Glasgow was little more than a two-hour run. The traffic cop who'd caught the black Alfa's number had just blown sky-high the blonde widow's story of taking David Stanley on that route-finding safari into the Welsh mountains. The Alfa could have been in the city within part of the area of time that mattered, the hours during which the throw of a switch had started her husband on the way to slow, agonising death.

Inspector Bradford cleared his throat. 'I thought you'd want to know — '

'You thought!' Thane slapped him on the shoulder. 'That's an understatement!'

They broke off for a moment as the start of Moss's meal arrived, a bowl of pale, anaemic tomato soup. He tasted it, then posed the question on his mind. 'Who do we go for, Colin — her or Stanley?'

'Take them together, but I'd say Stanley is the one we'll have to concentrate on. And don't ask me how security mixes with a take-over bid.' Thane pushed back his chair. 'What I've got to do now is get a clearance for us to head north after them.'

'This afternoon?' Moss disliked the idea.

'No, there's an overnight train, and I'd prefer it,' said Thane, a hard glint in his eyes. 'I'll have the local county force contact Stanley and let him know I'll be paying him a visit in the morning.'

'Let him know?' Moss spluttered on a spoonful of soup. 'Why?'

'So he has time to worry about it,' said Thane grimly. 'Plenty of time, Phil — the more the better.'

★　★　★

Few remaining railway routes in the world are so picturesquely beautiful as the last handful of loch and mountain fringed miles leading to Kyle of Lochalsh. The metal track runs like a thin thread of civilisation through country which is a summer paradise and a winter hell, edged by deer fences and mountain torrents.

155

Then, when it breaks through to the lonely north-west coast, the island of Skye lies across the sea to add its silhouette to the previous grandeur.

Warm, bright sunshine streamed in through the windows as the restaurant car attached to the overnight sleeper train from Glasgow thrummed along the rails. Colin Thane helped himself to a last cup of coffee and looked away from the passing spectacle to the less pleasing sight of his companion downing a large tablespoonful of liquid paraffin.

'Couldn't you have done that back in your berth?'

Moss swallowed, grimaced, and looked hurt. 'Doc Williams said I should take it after breakfast.'

Thane grunted. Though his berth had been comfortable enough he'd had little sleep as the train rumbled north. And even before he'd got aboard he'd had reason to be short on temper.

First there had been a struggle with Superintendent Donfoot before the latter would let him make the trip. The acting C.I.D. chief had preferred the idea of sending someone from Headquarters until Thane had thrown in the threat of a direct appeal to the Chief Constable. Then, when he'd tried to contact Commander Allowes, the Admiralty security man's office had been politely vague on the telephone. They couldn't say where the Commander might be, they might manage to pass a message to him . . .

Thane had swallowed his wrath and left a brief message which would bring Allowes more or less up to date. The friendlier reception on his next telephone call, to Rossshire police headquarters, only partly soothed his feelings — though the northern county force were happy to co-operate.

The rest had been routine, leaving just enough time to pack a bag, meet Phil Moss at the station and board their train for the eleven-hour journey.

Moss cleared his throat. They were nearing their destination, the train was beginning to slow, and the first outlying cottages of the little harbour town were appearing alongside the track.

'Colin, how do we tackle him?'

'Stanley?' Thane watched his own reflection in the window glass for a moment. 'Hit him with it, straight out.'

Moss nodded in slow agreement. He'd made his own assessment of the burly, bearded Hydrostat Drives director. Tough and confident he might be. But he'd had a full night in which to worry over their coming visit. One hammer-blow question might be

157

enough to crack through to the truth.

They collected their bags as the train pulled into the terminal then left it and looked around, sniffing the clean sea air. Further up the platform the big diesel locomotive was still purring while gulls flew overhead. A little way beyond, they could see the little car-ferry boats busy plying between the Kyle slipway and Skye across the water. The few other passengers from their train were already heading for the ticket barrier.

'Chief Inspector Thane?' The soft Highland voice belonged to a bald-headed, sun-tanned man in a worn tweed suit. He inspected them carefully, then introduced himself. 'Sergeant Kingsley, county police — I've a car waiting.'

They completed the introductions, then Kingsley led the way to the station car park. He loaded their bags into the rear of a cream Austin 1800 saloon and slid into the driving seat. Thane took the passenger seat beside him while Moss spread in comfort in the back.

'Well now, we've done as you asked, sir,' said Kingsley, taking time to light a heavy, black-bowled pipe. 'The Hydrostat team and the Ministry of Defence folk are all over at Glenelg, some staying in one of the hotels, the rest scattered around cottages and the like.'

He puffed on the pipe, and the blue, pungent smoke clouded the car's interior. 'I saw this Mr Stanley myself last night, and told him you were coming.'

'How'd he take it?' Thane wound his window down an inch or so in self-defence.

'Man, I'd say he was a wee bit perturbed.' Sergeant Kingsley sucked again at his pipe, leaned forward, and key-started the car. 'We'd best be heading straight over, sir. Those tests they're doing will have started by now — 8 a.m. was the time they told me. We've about an hour's run ahead, south and west.'

'Any other car tests going on?' queried Moss.

Kingsley smiled a little as he began driving. 'Not the Ministry kind, Inspector. But there's always some make or other playin' around with their latest toys. Live up here and you never need to go to a motor show — you've seen it all a long time before. Right now there's a bunch of Frenchmen up in the hills wi' three queer-looking wee vans, drivin' them around like scalded cats. Then the Sunbeam folk are testing a new sports car near Inverness — ach, we get them all the time.'

Their journey took fractionally longer than the hour, despite the fast, confident style in which the county sergeant handled the car.

Once clear of the little town the road quickly narrowed as it wound through progressively wilder country and soon became a narrow single track with only occasional passing places. Often they were running beside an unfenced edge with a long drop down to the rocks and sea beneath.

'Eilean Donan castle.' Kingsley took one hand from the wheel and used his pipestem as a pointer. The old stronghold, standing out in the water at the end of a causeway, had a sprinkling of tourists prowling its base. Further along, grey herons stalked in the shallows of Loch Duich, where the green grass reaching down to the shore was speckled with shaggy, long-haired Highland cattle.

'And now there's a wee bit of a climb,' he told them a mile or two on, as they passed a handful of cottages.

Moss swallowed at the words. 'We've been doing nothing else,' he protested.

'Ach, that was just a wee rise or two in the ground,' declared the county man placidly. 'This is Mam Rattachan, a halfway decent climb.'

They soon saw what he meant. The pass ahead was an immediate, savage climb through thick forest and a winding series of blind hairpin bends. The car's engine bellowed in low gear and, while Kingsley concentrated on his task, Thane looked back at the rapidly shrinking lochside far below.

'This kind of road is a testbed on its own,' he said thoughtfully.

'It's used a lot,' agreed Kingsley, the pipe between his teeth. 'I read once how that Doctor Johnson fellow described the Mam Rattachan as 'a terrible steep to climb' — and he was right.' He grinned briefly. 'Still, there's worse around, the Applecross road for one. That's where the final runs are scheduled, for the day after tomorrow.'

The minutes passed, still the car climbed, and then at last they were at the crown of the pass. Kingsley drew the Austin to a halt on a narrow verge of moorland beside a trickle of crystal-clear water. All around and below them spread a green-brown panorama of hills and mountains.

'Down there,' he said briefly, pointing ahead. 'Where the trees end.'

Thane nodded, seeing the thread-like track which ran from the road towards a stretch of rough, uphill slope. A quarter way up the slope, dust rose from behind a steadily moving vehicle. Lower down, the sun glinted on other vehicles. The Hydrostat tests were under way.

Sergeant Kingsley brought them there in a

few fast, down-hill minutes and an odour of scorched brake-linings. The Austin parked beside a canvas-roofed Land-Rover with War Department badges on its doors, and they stepped out on a surface which seemed an equal mixture of bracken and loose, broken rock.

Thane looked up the slope and gave a soft whistle. The whole uphill climb seemed studded with rocky outcrops, stray boulders, old tree stumps and that vicious blend of bracken and gravel. The 'ghost' truck had come to a stop about halfway up — but the stop seemed a scheduled part of the test. As he watched, a flag waved and the vehicle's wheels began turning again.

'Those Ministry characters are making it tough,' mused Moss at his elbow.

A handful of men stood beside the cluster of vehicles drawn up near the test hill start line. But if they'd seen the police car arrive they gave no sign. Their attention was fixed on that squat, compact truck, its engine growling low as it moved in uncanny, almost fly-like fashion between the lines of white marker tapes which traced a vicious route to the top. Spaced along the way stood Ministry men in dustcoats and calf-length rubber boots, men who glanced briefly at stop-watches or ticked the papers on their clipboards as the truck went past.

'Colin.' Moss gave him a sudden nudge. Peter Hayston had just emerged from one of the start-line vehicles. The small, rabbit-faced works manager wore a bright red wool shirt with bleached cotton slacks, and as he noticed them he stood where he was, undecided.

Thane beckoned him over and he came slowly, almost reluctantly.

'Where's David Stanley?' asked Thane without preamble.

Hayston blinked at them through his spectacles then pointed up towards the truck, its engine sounding louder as it took a savage bend where the tapes snaked between two outcrops of rock. 'He's driving. If — if you want him, we're breaking for a spell once he gets to the top.'

Thane looked at the slope, sighed and glanced at Moss. 'Feel like some exercise, Phil?'

'Up there, on foot?' Moss was unhappy at the prospect.

'Och, it's not far,' encouraged Sergeant Kingsley. 'If you were a postman in these parts you'd climb worse every day.'

'Thanks.' Moss gave him a brief, baleful glare.

Hayston was still with them. 'It's a surprise

to find you up here, Chief Inspector,' he said awkwardly. 'Has something — I mean, are you any further forward? Can you say who killed Mr Carter?'

'We're beginning to make progress,' said Thane briefly. 'Everyone happy with the tests?'

'It's early yet. But I'd say everything's fine so far. The car's already finished its first run.' The works manager shuffled his feet. 'I'm working the field 'phone link to the top. I should — '

'We won't keep you.' Thane turned away from him. 'Sergeant, you can stay here. Keep an eye on things. Phil, let's get this mountaineering bit over with.'

They left the county man and set off. It was a long climb, even longer than it looked, and Thane soon had sweat furrowing down from his brow and running between his shoulderblades. Phil Moss followed doggedly, but the gap between them grew wider despite his panting efforts.

They were still only halfway up when the truck reached the top of the slope and its engine stopped. By the time Thane toiled up beside it and took the chance of a brief rest until Moss arrived, the finish line was deserted and the last of the group of observers were disappearing into two big shelter tents pitched about thirty yards along the slope.

'Don't ask me to do that again — not unless you're ready to carry me.' Moss staggered the last few steps to the truck and leaned wearily against its dusty side. Nearby, equally dust-covered, the Hydrostat ghost car lay parked and empty.

'You're in no danger,' Thane assured him. 'Let's have a look at these things.'

He moved round to the truck's cab and peered in. It was disappointingly normal, only the absence of a gear lever and the presence of a couple of extra dash panel gauges, along with the big, centrally hinged accelerator pad, marking it out from the usual. Underneath the chassis, however, was a different story. The usual heavy drive shaft and its auxiliaries were absent. Instead, a network of thin pipes led from a bulge near the engine area to small cylinders positioned at each wheel.

Feet crunched towards them over the loose gravel, and he turned.

'Not much to see, I'm afraid.' Ian Shaw stood by the tail of the vehicle, his overalls oil-stained, a cigarette hanging loose between his lips. The red-haired youngster was tired-eyed and somehow cautious, despite his faint grin. 'I saw you coming up. Didn't anyone tell you there's a service track over on the far side? You could have thumbed a lift up with somebody.'

'They didn't.' Moss swore briefly but fluently, and glared back down the way he'd come.

'Well, now you know.' Shaw showed his enjoyment of the situation and came a few steps nearer. 'I heard from — well, on the grapevine that you were coming north, Chief Inspector. Satisfied yet that I told you the truth about Sunday?'

Thane looked at him for a moment then nodded. 'Part of it checks. That doesn't mean we're completely happy.' He saw the young mechanic flush, but didn't pursue the point. 'Where do we find David Stanley?'

'Over in the main tent.' Shaw thumbed in its direction. 'And I've got work to do — mind if I get on with it?' Without waiting for an answer he took a long, slim-jawed wrench from one pocket of his overalls and slid in beneath the truck's chassis.

They moved on, hearing a low buzz of voices as they neared the largest of the tents.

Inside, a rough dozen of people were standing around sipping coffee from plastic cups. Four others, all strangers, one in army uniform with major's insignia, sat at a small table in one corner, papers spread around them.

166

The rest — Thane ticked faces off against his mental list. Stanley was there, his burly, bearded figure prominent at the hub of the gathering. Lynne Carter's blonde head was close by his side, and the widow was listening to an enthusiastic, arm-waving Bart Kelly. The only other woman in the group was Jane Maulden. She presided by the coffee urn, trim and petite in a grey brushed wool sweater and slacks.

Her current customer was a surprise. Commander Allowes, red-faced, perspiring, turned as others saw the two arrivals and the buzz of conversation died. He laid down his cup with care and came towards them.

''Morning, Thane,' he said quietly. 'I got your message.'

Thane grunted. 'That's something, at any rate. Your office didn't tell me you'd be here.'

'I wouldn't expect them to,' parried the security man easily, his voice dropping to a murmur. 'I'm here for a reason. But it's not within your province, not yet anyway.' He fell silent as Stanley pushed his way towards them, Lynne Carter close behind him. She'd abandoned any pretence at widow's weeds and wore a dark brown shirt-blouse with pale blue linen slacks, their tops tucked into a fashion designer's version of lightweight desert boots.

'Glad to see you,' said Stanley, his voice loud and earnest. 'I've been wondering when you'd show up and tell what this 'urgent inquiry' business is about.' He frowned heavily. 'If it helps nail the thug who murdered Bill Carter — '

'It might. We've made some progress.' Thane glanced at the woman by Carter's side. There were lines of strain beneath her make-up and her eyes met his with something close to apprehension. 'Mrs Carter, I want to talk to you and Mr Stanley — privately. Outside, I think.'

'Right,' declared Stanley. He waved Jane Maulden over and told her, 'Keep an eye on these Ministry characters in case they need help with their arithmetic. But Jane, don't let them land you with work — you're on my payroll, not one of their mob.'

She nodded and crossed towards the foursome's table. Commander Allowes had already begun a tactful withdrawal in the direction of the coffee urn. But another interruption took shape.

'Hey, David — ' Kelly gave Thane a cheerful nod as he shoved forward. 'I'm not butting in. Just that if nobody needs me for a spell I'll head off down the hill and 'phone back to my office.' The public relations man grimaced as he explained for the Millside

168

men's benefit. 'Some bright boy planned things so that the only outside exchange 'phone in this place is back at the start line.'

'Go ahead,' said Stanley absently. He sighed as Kelly went out, then touched Lynne Carter's arm and glanced at the two detectives. 'Right, let's get it over with.'

Thane led the way from the tent and along the slope until they reached a grey-white boulder well out of earshot. 'This will do.'

'Well?' Stanley face was expressionless. The breeze blew a wisp of hair across Lynne Carter's face and she brushed it away with a quick, nervous hand.

Thane eyed them coldly. 'We want the truth this time.'

'What do you mean?' There was a hoarse edge to Stanley's voice.

'You told me that you spent most of Sunday driving around some mountains in Wales,' said Phil Moss almost wearily. 'You said you didn't leave them until late in the evening.'

Thane nodded. 'Which makes it difficult to explain how your car went through a Carlisle police checkpoint in the afternoon, heading north for Glasgow — heading north at a time when you say you were more than two hundred miles to the south.'

Lynne Carter bit hard on her lip, her

colour heightening. Stanley said nothing for a moment, then turned towards her. 'Lynne?'

She shut her eyes and nodded. 'Tell them, David. There's nothing else to do.'

'That's sensible,' agreed Thane softly, leaning back against the rock.

Stanley combed the fingers of one hand through his beard, then shrugged. 'All right, we lied. And we hoped we'd get away with it — but it's got nothing to do with Bill Carter's death or anything else that's happened at the plant.'

'No?' Thane waited.

'Lynne and I, we — ' Stanley broke off, his face twisting as he groped for words. 'Look, do I have to spell it out?'

She silenced him with a shake of her head. 'What he's trying to say, Mr Thane, is that we did get back early. We stopped at a little place outside the city and — well, we were together that night. It had happened before.' The tension seemed to drain from her face as she spoke. What replaced it was hard to define, but was far removed from fear. 'If that makes me a bitch I'm sorry. But we didn't go near my husband or the plant.'

'I see.' Thane made an effort to control his feelings. 'Where were you?'

'A hotel. They'll remember us.' Lynne Carter said it simply, her husky voice low.

'We — we've been there before.'

'But it's not like it sounds,' grated Stanley. 'Look, Thane, she had a rough time from Carter.'

'It probably doesn't interest him,' she said quietly.

'It definitely does,' corrected Thane. 'Did Carter have any idea this was going on?'

Stanley shook his head. 'No. And I don't think he'd have worried too much. He treated Lynne like a piece of window dressing, handy to have around.'

'The kind of window dressing he'd give a controlling interest?'

'In the company?' Stanley growled. 'That was early on — I don't think he realised what he'd done till later. Then he tried to get it back.'

'There's a phrase for it, Chief Inspector.' Lynne Carter bit lightly on her lower lip. 'Marry in haste, repent at leisure. For six months everything seemed fine. Then — it just died, that's all. Don't ask me whose fault it was, because I don't know.'

Phil Moss scuffed one foot along the ground. 'There must have been some kind of a reason, Mrs Carter.'

'Have you a wife?' she asked. As he shook his head she gave a faint imitation of a smile. 'Then it's hard to explain. He wasn't cruel, he didn't try to hurt me. Afterwards, well, I wasn't an angel and David was — '

'Handy?' Moss tried to appear sympathetic and failed.

Stanley growled, his hands clenched by his side. 'What matters is we didn't kill him.'

'Even though he was blocking a take-over offer that gave you the chance of another kind of killing?' Thane leaned forward, watching the effect of the words.

Amazingly, Stanley laughed. 'That? You mean — hell, it was the other way round.' He rammed fist against palm. 'The first time D.R. Engineering made a bid we threw it out, straight away. But this last time he was the one who suddenly changed his mind. It was Carter who wanted to sell, Lynne and I who were stopping him.'

It was Thane's turn to stir the loose gravel at his feet while he tried to think, to keep pace with the complete turnround. 'Who else knew about it? Hayston, or your secretary?'

'Jane?' Stanley shook his head. 'Nobody was told. It was our business, ours alone.'

'Why did you take the desk diary from Carter's room?'

'His what — ?' Stanley was puzzled.

'The appointment book,' prompted Moss.

Still puzzled, Stanley glanced at Lynne Carter. She shook her head.

'We didn't touch it,' he said briefly. 'Does it matter?'

'Somebody thinks so,' growled Thane. 'And the same somebody must be very grateful for the way you've had us chasing our tails.'

Stanley sighed, took out his cigarettes, gave one to the blonde, then shielded a match for her. He lit his own and drew hard on it. 'I suppose so. But can you blame us, Thane? For a start, think how the newspapers would treat it — husband murdered while wife and partner share love nest.' He grimaced. 'When Lynne heard Bill was dead we decided to keep our mouths shut. I had those notes for the Welsh test route, we weren't involved — it seemed to make sense.'

Behind them, a starter whined and the truck's engine burst to life. They turned to watch. The engine revved high for a few moments then died. The cab door opened, Ian Shaw clambered out, and as the door slammed shut again he strode off towards the tents.

'How much do you know about Shaw?' queried Thane.

Stanley was happy to change the subject. 'He's a good worker and he knows his stuff. It's just as well we've got him, too — we had a spot of trouble with one of the drive pipes this morning, and he's the fellow who sorted it out.' He gazed affectionately at the two test vehicles. 'At least that's going well. The Ministry observers were happy enough about the car's performance, but the truck made out even better. She came up that slope like it didn't exist. You know why, Thane? Because there's almost no mechanical friction loss — up to twenty per cent of any conventional vehicle's power is used up that way before the road wheels turn. But not with fluid drive, and remember it is individual drive to each wheel.'

'I saw you go up,' said Thane with scant interest.

'Where we've got everyone licked is in the relief valve control layout, those packages at the wheel units. They're — ' Stanley stopped and pursed his lips regretfully. 'Sorry. You don't want the sales talk.'

'I asked about Shaw,' said Thane frostily. 'Did you know he had a quarrel with Carter last Friday?'

Stanley blinked. 'No — Hayston just told me Bill Carter had spoken to Shaw, and that there was still some problem about how much we'd pay him. Who says there was a quarrel?'

Thane shook his head. 'It doesn't matter. But something else does now that we've squeezed the truth from you two. The security leakage from the plant — '

'If it happened.' Stanley's manner was faintly cynical. 'I'd like some proof.'

'We've got proof,' Thane told him bluntly. 'The time-lock on the plant safe had been rigged, a professional job. Anyone who had the combination could swing it open whenever he wanted.' He glanced at Lynne Carter. 'He — or she.'

There was a long silence. Somewhere in the hills, far away, the sound carried on the breeze, a dog was barking.

'I didn't know,' said Stanley at last, his voice bitter. 'I thought they'd just been working on the same lines and come up with the same answers.' He took a deep breath. 'Hell, I fought them in Korea — but I never thought they'd pop up in my own backyard!'

Lynne Carter dropped her cigarette and ground it out under her foot. 'Mr Thane, are you saying Bill's death was — well, because someone was trying to get hold of more information?'

Thane nodded. 'It sounds wild, but it could have happened.' He frowned, reluctant to go too far with them. 'I'm interested in Shaw — and in why Peter Hayston should be more than ordinarily friendly with him.'

'Hayston? That useless deadhead?' Stanley scratched his beard. 'We've been carrying him as works manager because Bill Carter wanted it that way. Believe me, he won't last long in the job — not now.'

Moss cleared his throat, feeling rather out of things. 'Who'll take his place?'

Stanley shrugged. 'I don't know yet. But he's no good. Bill Carter kept him on because they used to work together, before Bill started out on his own. Otherwise — well, I'd say even Bill didn't think much of him.' A new thought struck him. 'Look, if you're so keen to find this appointment book, why not ask Hayston about it? The story I got was that he was in that office and going through Bill's desk five minutes after they'd found the body.'

'Hayston said he needed some production schedules,' mused Thane. 'I was there at the time.'

'Production schedules?' Stanley snorted at the idea. 'Here's something else — funny how pieces fall in place once you start. We've got Bart Kelly along to do the general P.R. stuff on this test. But we didn't always have Kelly on call. In the early days, when the firm was starting, Hayston did any publicity work we needed — and that included photographs.' He stuck his thumbs in the waistband of his trousers, a glowering, angry figure. 'And Hayston always knew the safe combination

— it adds up, doesn't it?'

Thane's mouth hardened and he looked down the slope towards the vehicles at the start line. The whole situation had swung, swung at a speed which made it hard to keep pace.

'Mr Thane — ' Lynne Carter stepped close to him, her voice pleading. 'About David and I — does everyone need to know?'

He shrugged. 'We'll check your story. If it's true, that's it finished. Except' — he turned to Stanley — 'do you know your blood group?'

Stanley frowned. 'No, I did, but I can't remember. If it's important — '

'No.'

'We — we've already talked things over,' volunteered Lynne Carter. She stepped nearer to Stanley, one hand reaching for his. 'We'll have to let a few months pass, for decency. But after that we'll be married. I thought — well, that you should know.'

Thane nodded, in no particular mood to begin congratulations. 'Phil — '

'Down?' queried Moss.

'Down.' He rasped the word. Peter Hayston was going to have something to be nervous about when they arrived.

6

They came back down the slope the easy way, passengers in a Land-Rover driven by one of the Ministry observers who had business at the start-line.

Sergeant Kingsley was still sunning himself beside the police car, and he pulled himself erect as they approached, a faint smile on his lips.

'Get what you wanted, sir?' he asked.

'What we wanted, but not what we expected,' said Thane cryptically. 'I spoke to a man in a red wool shirt when we arrived here. Any idea where he is now?'

'The wee fellow with glasses?' Kingsley nodded. 'Aye, he drove off in an old station wagon just a moment or so back.'

Thane swore softly and looked around.

'There's Kelly,' said Moss, pointing towards one of the nearby supply trucks. 'Let's try him.'

They hurried over. Bart Kelly was sitting on the truck's running board, his eyes half-closed, a field telephone box cradled in his lap and the cable snaking away from beside his feet.

'Hello again — ' he yawned as they approached, moved the box from his lap, and rose lazily to his feet. 'Finished up there?'

'We're looking for Hayston,' rapped Thane. 'Where's he gone?'

Kelly blinked. 'He won't be long. He borrowed my car and went back to change his clothes. He was fooling around with a can of oil, and ended up spilling most of it over himself.'

Thane gestured towards the field telephone. 'Nobody rang through on that thing from the finish line?'

'No.' Kelly was puzzled. 'But I said I'd man it till he got back.'

'Back from where?' demanded Moss.

'The cottage — a rented place we're sharing. There wasn't room in the hotel and — '

Thane cut him short. 'Like to take us there?'

'If it can't wait. But the place is only a couple of miles down the road — '

They led him over to Sergeant Kingsley's car, climbed aboard and set off, Kelly directing from the rear seat. From the main road, they soon struck off on another track almost hidden by trees.

'What's going on?' asked Kelly with an edge of curiosity. 'Don't tell me you've an interest in Hayston. He's the kind who jumps at his own shadow.'

'Let's just say we want to talk to him,' said Thane briefly.

'Talk?' Kelly rubbed his chin. 'That's what my old mother would call 'keep your fingers out of the pie and they won't be burned.'' He tapped Kingsley on the shoulder. 'There's a farm road going off to the right at that old tree on ahead. Take it.'

Kingsley nodded and slowed for the turn — then a flat, angry blast, close at hand, hit their ears. Sheer instinct made him brake hard, throwing his passengers forward, while the explosion died in a muffled rumble and a dark cloud rose above the trees. He recovered, swore, and his foot rammed down on the accelerator.

A hundred yards down the pot-holed farm track they entered a clearing. The cottage lay to one side, Kelly's old estate car parked outside its door. But the small whitewashed building's windows were so much shattered glass, part of the rusted corrugated iron roof had collapsed inward, and the last of the dust and debris was still settling.

'God Almighty — ' Kelly's mouth hung open.

They stopped beside the estate car, piled out, and headed for the cottage door. It was still locked. Thane took a half-step back, swung his foot, and his heel connected with pile-driving accuracy at a point just below the keyhole. The door burst open and they stared into the hallway. At the far end, an inner door lay against the wall, blown from its hinges.

'That's his room — ' Kelly started forward, but Phil Moss hauled him back.

'We get paid for this,' said Moss cynically. 'Civilians last in line.'

They moved cautiously down the hallway. At its end, the little bedroom was a shambles, a hole blown through ceiling and roof, sunlight beaming through to give life to the thick, dust-filled air. Over by the window, beside the shattered remains of an old chest of drawers, a figure in that vivid red shirt lay crumpled on the floor.

'Wait.' Thane crossed over on his own. Peter Hayston was lying face down, but there was no need to turn him over to know he was dead. Splintered wood lay all around, and Thane's lips tightened as he saw the shattered, twisted casing of a small metal box lying among the debris. He glanced around. Other fragments of the metal were scattered around the room, embedded in the plaster walls, in the wood of the bed's headboard, even in the ceiling.

'Phil — ' Thane beckoned his second-in-command forward. Together, they gently eased Hayston's body on its side, then wished they hadn't as they saw the full effect of the blast. The booby-trap bomb might have been small, but it had been powerful. What little of his clothing remained was burned and scorched, but the dark, thick oil-stain was still visible on the front of his slacks.

They lowered him again. Moss stood up, his feet crunching on part of the man's broken spectacles. In the doorway, Sergeant Kingsley and Kelly stood silent. Kingsley moistened his lips.

'No sense in an ambulance, sir?'

'None,' said Thane quietly. 'Phil, take a look around. And be careful.'

'He'd a suitcase under the bed,' volunteered Kelly from the doorway.

Moss crossed over. The foot of the bed had collapsed, but when he peered under he could see the outline of the case. He reached in, found the handle, and pulled it free with a grunt. He glanced round, saw Thane making a slow, grim-faced search of the dead man's pockets, and laid the suitcase on top of the mattress. The locks clicked open, he lifted the lid, then stared, mesmerised, at the small box which lay within.

'Get down!' Kelly broke the spell, hurling from the doorway in a flying tackle which took Moss at knee level and sent him tumbling to the floor. At the same instant Thane threw himself flat beside Hayston's body and had a momentary impression of Sergeant Kingsley still standing open-mouthed in the doorway.

There was an orange flash, an ear-blasting explosion, and a vicious spatter of fragmented debris. Plaster and lathing rained down from the already shattered ceiling then, with a screech and a groan, an entire section of the corrugated roof crashed into the room. Thane felt a heavy blow strike across his back, couldn't move, and knew a moment's panic until he finally jerked free of the section of roof beam which had pinned him down. He staggered to his feet, the taste of plaster dust and acrid explosives fumes in his mouth and lungs.

'Phil — ' the name came from his lips in a hoarse appeal.

He heard a groan, traced it to beneath the corrugated iron, and tore the heavy sheeting aside. Moss groaned again and rose shakily to his knees. Blood trickled from a gash on his forehead and he stared at Thane, dazed and shaken. Then his eyes widened.

'Where's Kelly?'

'Over here,' croaked the P.R. man's voice. 'I can't get up.'

Together, they found the man. He was lying over by the wall, jammed against it by another of the roof beams. As they eased it off him he winced with pain.

'Take it easy.' He shook his head as they tried to lift him. 'Give me a minute — I feel like there's something broken inside me.'

Thane remembered Kingsley. 'Stay with him, Phil — ' he struggled back across the debris to the hallway then leaned against the doorway and sighed with relief. The county sergeant, his tanned face blackened, part of his jacket torn loose, was already staggering to his feet.

'All right, Sergeant?'

'Och, I think so, sir,' said Kingsley slowly. 'But the last time that happened to me there was a war going on an' it made more sense.'

The grey humour in the words helped. Thane nodded and turned back into the room, where Bart Kelly was now sitting upright, one arm held protectively across his chest.

Kelly wheezed, coughed, and shook his head. 'I'd say we were damned lucky!'

'Lucky?' Phil Moss took a deep breath. 'Any luck that was going was thanks to you.'

The P.R. man shrugged then winced. 'All

— all I'll say is I want to know what's going on.'

'We'd discovered that Hayston might have the answers to some awkward questions,' said Thane, moving cautiously round the room, pushing the cluttered debris aside with his feet. 'Somebody else must have had the same idea.' He searched on, frowning.

'Lost something?' queried Kelly.

Thane nodded bitterly. He'd lost a chance, lost it by little more than a minute, the short length of time by which Hayston had beaten them to the cottage. But there was the other side of that coin. If they'd been with Hayston when the first, unexpected booby-trap bomb had exploded . . .

'Kelly, how many people knew you and Hayston were living here?'

'Just about everyone,' said Kelly. 'The accommodation was allocated before we set out. Getting a place like this seemed okay — the owners are off on holiday somewhere.'

They had a surprise coming, thought Thane. 'Had any visitors?'

'Nope. And we drove out to the test slope together this morning.' Kelly gnawed his lip. 'I'll tell you this. Dave Stanley's secretary is one lucky girl.'

'Eh?' Phil Moss had a bismuth tablet in his mouth. He moved it to one cheek. 'Why?'

185

'Because she came out here later on.' Kelly saw their faces and shook his head. 'Look, it was simple enough. I was at the start line and found I'd left a stopwatch behind. Jane saved me the trip back — she was going that way, on some errand of her own. I asked her, she said yes, I gave her a key, and I got my watch.'

'Where was the watch?' asked Thane, frowning.

'Not in here, thank heaven. I left it on the dressing table in my own room.' Bart Kelly winced impatiently. 'Look, Thane, how about getting me to a doctor? I'd like to know what's happened to my insides.'

★ ★ ★

More than an hour had to pass before Thane had a chance to see Jane Maulden. First — and surprisingly, by his wrist-watch, only a few scant minutes after the second blast though it seemed an age longer — a car came bouncing along the track to the cottage clearing followed by another, then a truck, all from the test slope, all laden with would-be rescuers.

Commander Allowes and David Stanley were in the lead car. While Sergeant Kingsley held the rest back, the two men inspected the scene with Thane. Allowes was quiet, but with a cold glint in his small blue eyes. Stanley, however, stared around him with barely controlled amazement.

'We heard the noise and thought it sounded — ah — interesting,' murmured Allowes. 'I must admit I'd certain doubts about what we'd find.'

'Damn the pretty speeches!' Stanley was flushed and angry, his own previous discomfiture forgotten. 'That's Hayston lying there — and I want somebody to tell me why. Come on, one of you. Why would anyone set up this — this devil's mousetrap for a harmless little weed like him?'

Thane shrugged. 'You gave me a couple of good reasons before I went looking for him,' he reminded the Hydrostat boss. 'Somebody else must have had them in mind.'

'A pity you didn't get to him first,' said Allowes with what could have been a slight edge of annoyance. He examined one of the shattered bomb cases with tender interest. 'Of course, he had an alibi for Sunday's affair, but for the rest, he was probably the contact man — at least the contact man.'

'That kind of hindsight comes easy.' Thane knew an increasing, gnawing impatience at the security man's easy criticism. 'Your people were the ones who gave him a security clearance.'

'It happens.' Allowes winced a little and looked again at the body on the floor. He lifted a blanket from the scattered bedding and spread it carefully over Hayston's form. He regarded the result with distaste. 'Two of these contraptions in the one room — well, whoever he was, he certainly wanted to make sure of things. Checked the rest of the place?'

Phil Moss answered, coming through from the hallway. 'It's clean,' he said briefly. He threw Thane a brief, significant glance. 'Kelly's room hasn't been touched and there's nothing there to help us. The kitchen's pretty well intact, Colin.'

They went through. It was a small, whitewashed room with an old-fashioned cooking range, a table and some chairs. The shelves held crockery and a few tins and though some of the cups and plates had been shattered by the blast and the window-glass had disappeared there was no other sign of damage.

Thane let himself slump into one of the chairs. There was a nagging ache running down his back and legs to remind him of how he'd been pinned by that beam. 'Where's Kelly?'

'Outside,' said Moss. 'He felt like some air. Sergeant Kingsley's radioed for an ambulance and advised his headquarters.'

'Good.' Thane eased himself in the chair. 'Where's the nearest telephone?'

'Around here?' Moss raised an expressive eyebrow. 'What do we do about Hayston's body?'

'Move it. Let's hope Kelly won't mind sharing the ride.'

Stanley gave a grunt. 'I thought you fellows didn't touch anything until the experts arrived.'

'The experts are here,' reminded Allowes dryly. 'They've — ah — first-hand knowledge of what happened.'

'I've asked for a fingerprint team to come out,' said Thane coldly. He turned towards Stanley. 'What happens now as far as you're concerned?'

'You mean the tests?' Stanley gave a faint groan. 'Hell knows — I suppose the decent thing is to call them off for the rest of the day.'

'Keep them going,' advised Commander Allowes blandly. 'Give your people something to do. You'd prefer it anyway, wouldn't you?'

Stanley gave a reluctant nod. 'Being cold-blooded about it, yes. But what about here — need any help, Thane?'

'Later,' said Thane slowly. 'Take the rest of your people back for now. But I'd be glad if you'd send Jane Maulden over in about an hour.'

'Jane?' Stanley showed his surprise. 'Why?'

'Kelly says she was out here this morning.'

'I'll send her,' agreed Stanley wearily. He seemed about to comment on it, but shrugged instead. 'What about you, Commander?'

Allowes glanced at Thane and gave a faintly apologetic smile. 'Nothing much I can do either,' he declared. 'I'll ride back with you.'

They'd been gone some time before the ambulance arrived — an elderly vehicle, kept in a local garage and manned by the garage owner and his son. Sergeant Kingsley supervised its loading — Hayston's body on one side, a slightly unwilling Kelly on the other — then, as it drove off, turned to Thane.

'Aye, and now we can get on wi' the work, eh, sir?'

Thane nodded, and led the way back into the cottage kitchen. On the table, lying in a handkerchief, was the small pile of personal items he'd removed from the dead works manager's pockets. Phil Moss perched himself alongside.

'What now?' he demanded.

'Plenty,' said Thane grimly. 'Sergeant, when do you expect your lads to arrive?'

190

'Well, not for a wee spell,' admitted Kingsley. 'Headquarters say the local constable's gone out on a sheep-stealing report, but they're trying to locate him. There's a car on its way from Kyle with a couple of men, and they shouldn't be too long. The fingerprint van — ' he shrugged. 'It's got a long way to come, sir.'

'Right.' Thane nodded. 'Phil, what's our state in here?'

'When I said Kelly's room was clean I meant it,' said Moss in matter-of-fact fashion. 'I went through his stuff down to the last shirt-button.'

'There's still the station wagon outside,' reminded Thane. 'But we'll start with the rest of this place — and that includes gathering up every fragment we can of those two bomb-cases. After that, take a look around the edge of the clearing — vehicle tracks, anything else you can find.'

'Aye, fine, sir.' Sergeant Kingsley had been prowling the kitchen. 'Did you notice this was in the place?' Gently, respectfully, he laid an almost full bottle of whisky on the table. 'I was thinking, sir, maybe we should have a wee fortification first.' He moistened his lips at the thought. 'You could call it medicinal, I'd say — after all, it's not every day I get damned near blown out of my clothes.'

191

Thane looked at the county man's earnest face and chuckled. 'It's your area, not mine, Sergeant. Let's see if you can find three cups.'

* * *

The cottage and the estate car checked, a much more cheerful Moss and Kingsley were roaming the fringe of the clearing when a familiar grey car nosed its way quietly along the track and stopped a few yards from the cottage door where Thane stood watching. He saw the girl climb out from the passenger side, then gave a grunt of surprise as the driver emerged.

Whatever attitude they'd adopted in the past, Jane Maulden and Ian Shaw now seemed on friendly enough terms. They stood where they were for a moment, fascinated by the sight of the wrecked roof and shattered windows then, the girl's face pale, Shaw's expression a tight mask, they walked towards him.

'I heard you'd been lucky, Chief Inspector,' said Shaw with an unfamiliar gravity. 'I'd say they were right.'

'Hayston could have used some of that luck.' Thane thumbed towards the car. 'I thought the test programme was going on.'

'It is,' agreed Shaw. 'David Stanley had a

session with the Ministry men and they're going ahead. But the truck's the main interest for the moment, so I borrowed this. Anyway it keeps the engine warm and the fluid system happy.'

'Shaw, I'd like you to wait,' said Thane. 'Jane, we'll talk in the cottage.'

The girl hesitated and her eyes showed her reluctance. Shaw moved a little closer to her and frowned. 'Now wait — '

'Alone,' said Thane steadily. 'There's nothing inside to worry about — not now.'

She relaxed a little, understanding. 'It's all right, Ian. I'll go.'

'If you're sure.' Shaw gave a slow, unwilling nod. 'I'll stay by the car.' He turned on his heel and paced determinedly back the way he'd come.

Thane beckoned the girl. She followed him through to the kitchen and took the chair he indicated.

'You can guess why I want to see you, Jane?'

Her lips tightened a little. 'It wasn't difficult.'

He saw her eyes stray to the table where the little collection of Hayston's effects lay beside the whisky bottle. Leaning forward, he wrapped the items in the handkerchief and stuffed the bundle into his pocket. Then he pulled another of the chairs out from the table and sat down opposite her. 'Tell me about it.'

'There's not much to tell,' she declared. 'All the way over with Ian I've been trying to remember anything unusual, anything that seemed wrong. But everything was just — well, ordinary. When Bart Kelly heard I had to go back down to the hotel — '

'Time?'

She thought for a moment. 'About eight, I suppose, just as the tests were starting. We got the Ministry people settled, then Mr Stanley asked me to drive over and collect some papers he'd forgotten.'

'Everybody seems to have been forgetful this morning,' commented Thane dryly.

Jane Maulden flushed to the roots of her jet black hair. 'We'd a long drive yesterday, Chief Inspector, then a lot of last-minute preparation until late on.' She shrugged. 'Anyway, Bart Kelly told me about the stopwatch and gave me his key. I collected the papers, then looked in at the cottage on the way back.' She anticipated his question. 'I suppose that would be about eight-thirty — he'd drawn a map, but even so I lost some time on the way — I took a wrong turning.'

'You were alone on the trip?'

She nodded. 'Yes, I'd borrowed one of the vans.'

'Did you see anyone near the cottage?'

'No — and in a place as lonely as this I'd remember if I had.' One hand was plucking lightly, nervously, at the neck of her sweater. 'I went in, I found the stopwatch — and that was that.'

'While you were here, did you look around the place?'

'Just a little,' she confessed. 'I — well, most people like looking round houses, don't they?'

'Jane, this is important. Did you look into any drawers or open a cupboard — do anything like that at all?'

'No, of course not.' The hand at the neck of her sweater tightened. 'The stopwatch was lying out on Bart Kelly's dressing-table. I just had to lift it.'

'All right.' He watched her closely. 'You're more friendly with Shaw than you used to be.'

'I suppose so.' She spoke carefully, choosing her words. 'It — we drove north together the way things worked out. He — he's not so bad.'

'But he had that row with Carter.'

'Yes.' She drew a deep breath. 'Perhaps it was — well, more of an argument. Maybe I made too much of it.'

'Maybe.' Thane toyed with the whisky bottle and noticed for the first time that it was now close on two-thirds empty. Sergeant Kingsley's idea of a 'fortification' was no small measure. 'I'm told Shaw seemed pretty friendly with Peter Hayston.'

'Ian gets on well with most people,' she retorted, her chin coming up.

Thane sighed, knowing he would get little more from the girl. 'One last thing, Jane. You told me Carter knew your father, was a family friend. Hayston had been with Carter a long time, and I wondered if he'd known your father, too.'

He could have sworn he saw a brief flicker of alarm in her eyes, but she shook her head. 'I don't think so. I — well, I never had much to do with Peter Hayston at the plant, even though he was works manager. Any letters or secretarial work he needed were taken care of by one of the typists.'

'That's it, then.' Thane rose to his feet and smiled encouragingly. 'Before you go, maybe you'll do three hungry coppers a favour. It's close on lunchtime, that stove's still working, and we could use some tea and sand-wiches — '

'And while I'm occupied with that little chore you'll be free to grill Ian?' She treated him to a scornful twist of her mouth. 'All

196

right, but I don't see how he can help you, Chief Inspector.'

'That's my problem, isn't it?' He gave her a faint smile. 'I'll try and find out.'

★ ★ ★

He found Shaw still waiting by the car, a scowl of concentration on his face as he tossed pebbles one by one off the back of his hand towards an old tin can he was using as a target.

Shaw glanced round briefly at the sound of his approach, flicked another pebble on its way, then turned his attention towards Thane.

'Where's Jane?'

'I asked her to give us a few minutes.' Thane folded his arms, his manner grim, his tall, broad figure overshadowing the stockily built young engineer. 'I want some answers from you, Shaw.'

'That's no surprise.' The soft Scots-Canadian drawl held a guarded sarcasm. Shaw placed another pebble on the back of his hand, flicked, and the stone clanged against the tin. 'Know the game, Chief Inspector? I learned it from an uncle — he spent three years of the depression sitting on a pit bing doing nothing else.' He stooped to pick up another pebble. 'First question, where have I been all morning, right? Well, I was on the hill, with plenty of witnesses around.'

'It helps,' agreed Thane. He waited until Shaw had the pebble balanced, ready to flick. 'How long had you known Hayston?'

Shaw jerked and the pebble flew wide. 'Now wait a minute — '

'How long?'

The younger man's attitude was suddenly more watchful, despite the attempted indifference in his voice. 'I went to the plant about two weeks back, looking for a job. Then I bumped into him in a bar in town a few nights later, we talked some more, and he fixed me an interview with Carter. That's all.'

'You're sure?'

'What you're forgetting is that I'm a hydrostatic specialist and unlike cops, they don't grow on trees.' Shaw thrust his hands in his pockets, still defiant. 'Save yourself some time, Thane. I haven't killed anyone, I don't want to kill anyone — and even Admiralty security aren't going to try and suggest I could be connected with the ruddy information leakages. Hell, I was still in Canada till a few weeks back!'

'Be glad of that,' said Thane softly. He reached into an inside pocket, extracted the little flashlight picture which was his souvenir of the brush with the Hydrostat plant intruder, and showed it to Shaw. 'Did Hayston take this?'

'How would I know?' grinned Shaw loosely. 'But it flatters you.'

'Hayston was handy with a camera, wasn't he?'

Shaw gave a faint shrug. 'If you say so — I can't argue.'

They stared at one another in silence, Thane grim and challenging, Ian Shaw bluntly unyielding. Then, at last, Shaw glanced away. 'If that's the lot it's time I got the car back. They'll be needing it.'

'You can go.' Thane sighed, and thumbed towards the cottage. 'Both of you.'

He stayed where he was while Shaw strode towards the little house. After a moment Shaw reappeared with the girl and they climbed back into the test car. As it started up and purred past him, Jane Maulden raised one hand in a vague farewell, her face troubled and her eyes filled with a strained indecision. Then the car had left the clearing, and the sound of its engine faded into the distance.

⋆ ⋆ ⋆

When Moss and Sergeant Kingsley returned to the cottage they found Thane sitting pensively at the kitchen table, the oddments from Hayston's pockets spread in front of him. He looked up as they entered.

'Well, Phil?'

'Nothing,' said Moss with disgust. 'I've been half-eaten by midges, I'm still picking thorns out of my hide, but there's no trace of anything out there — man, beast or tyre-track.' He rubbed his hands at the sight of the plate piled with sandwiches which sat a little to one side. 'Now that's a happy thought.'

'Miss Maulden's helping hand,' said Thane wryly. 'And that's about the extent of her co-operation. There's tea in that pot on the stove.'

'Tea, aye . . . ' Sergeant Kingsley was thoughtful. 'Well, if there's nothing better — '

'There isn't.'

The country man began pouring while Thane gave them a sketch of his conversations.

'Sounds like they're worried,' agreed Moss, reaching for a sandwich. 'But this happy friendship business is a surprise. I thought she'd given him the deep freeze treatment till now.'

'Maybe I've got the answer to that,' Thane

told him. He reached for Hayston's bundle, found what he wanted and held it for inspection. It was a small, faded, dog-eared photograph of four men standing against the side of an old car, four men in sports clothes, wide grins on their faces and a crate of beer by their feet. 'This was inside the back flap of Hayston's wallet, Phil. I missed it first time but — well, recognise anyone?'

'Eh?' Moss peered more closely. 'Uh-huh. This one on the left is Carter — a few years younger, but it's Carter.'

'Anyone else?'

Moss frowned. Two of the men were older and strangers but the other one, the youngest, a boy by comparison and probably still in his teens when the picture was taken was oddly familiar. 'Hell, make an allowance for the years and it could be Ian Shaw!'

'It could be,' agreed Thane happily. He turned to Sergeant Kingsley. 'How quickly could you get one of us back to Glasgow?'

Kingsley stroked his bald dome of a head. 'There's a flight, just the one daily, from Inverness to Glasgow. It leaves a bit after 5 p.m. and there's maybe a three-hour drive from here to Inverness — but we could make it, sir.'

'Then that's your job, Phil. The bomb fragments go to Dan Laurence's lab, and by

201

the time you've delivered them I'll have made a telephoned date for you with the city Inland Revenue office.'

'With who?' Moss stared blankly.

'Inland Revenue, the tax Daleks,' said Thane patiently. 'Phil, this has been nagging at me since yesterday, since we had that brush with Splits Clark — the only dividend we've had from that business. Remember how he moaned that we were only judging him on his record, not by what he'd been before his first conviction?'

'Yes, but — '

'Maybe we should do the same here — go back to before the beginning. Find out more about what Carter and the others were doing before this Hydrostat Drives firm was founded.'

'Fair enough, but the Inland Revenue — '

'Even tax collectors can be useful. Phil, they've records on file for every man and woman who ever earned a penny, records that make our own look like an amateur sideshow. Check back, use Carter and Hayston as your baselines. I want to know when they worked together on somebody's payroll, if Shaw was there at the same time — and if Jane Maulden's father could be one of the other men in that picture.'

'Right.' Moss drained the last of the tea in

his cup, took another two of the sandwiches in one hand, then regarded Thane suspiciously. 'What about you — what's your programme?'

Thane shrugged. 'Don't worry, I'll pass the time. And Phil — ' he grinned a little. 'Try and get the morning plane back, will you?'

His second-in-command's reply was short, sour, and blistering.

* * *

The first of the county men, a flustered local constable in a small patrol van, arrived moments after Kingsley's car had departed. Next came a car-load from Kyle and then, after a long gap, the promised fingerprint team pulled up at the cottage. Thane left them to it, and used Kelly's station wagon to find the nearest farmhouse with a telephone.

For the next two hours he was busy on the line. First on the list was the Inland Revenue office in Glasgow, to advise them what was needed. After that came Headquarters and an incredulous Superintendent Donfoot, followed by a similar call to the county authorities. He traced Bart Kelly to the local cottage hospital — located over at Broadfoot on the island of Skye. People weren't the only items thin on the ground in the north.

'The fellow seems to have had more than his share of luck,' mused the hospital's doctor over the wires. 'We patched him up a little and treated him for bruising and shock, but otherwise he's intact. I'll be sending him back by ambulance — though that's only a precaution.'

'And the p.m. on Hayston?' queried Thane. 'How soon can you manage it?'

'That's more difficult,' confessed the doctor. 'Our regular man isn't available. He's off on a fishing trip, and autopsies aren't my strongest point.'

It meant more telephone calls, ending with the arrangement that Professor MacMaster would come up from Glasgow — the University expert, impartial investigation as his stock in trade, could and did work for whom he chose.

At the finish, it was late dusk by the time Colin Thane reached the Glenpeak Arms, the big old-fashioned hotel which had become the test team's unofficial headquarters. They had only one room still available, three floors up — and the central heating pipes stopped on the floor below. But the bed was soft and clean, the window gave a view far out across the hills and, a northern rarity, there was a private bath attached.

He unpacked his bag, spent half an hour of

warm soaking in the tub, and climbed out with most of the aches gone from his limbs. Once he'd put on a clean shirt, had finished dressing and smoked a cigarette he felt pretty much his usual self.

Downstairs, he found the bar and ordered a whisky. As he drank it down he realised that, for the moment, there was only one other customer. An elderly man in heather-toned tweeds was over at a corner table with a lager and an opened book.

'Aye, we're quiet yet,' volunteered the barman. 'Most folk are still in the dining-room.'

'What about him?' queried Thane, laying his glass on the counter and nodding towards the corner.

'Mr Anderson?' The barman chuckled wisely. 'He's different. Comes in each night, orders one drink, then goes off to bed. But he'll be up at five and out chasing deer all over the hills before you or I have had breakfast. He's some kind of a naturalist.'

Thane grunted, then swung round as the bar door squeaked open.

'I thought you'd be here.' Bart Kelly grinned at him from the doorway, crossed over, and levered himself up into the next seat with deliberate care.

'How do you feel?' asked Thane.

'I'll mend now I've eaten,' said Kelly cheerfully. He ordered a gin then settled back with a sigh. 'Where's your shadow?'

'Moss?' Thane finished the rest of his whisky and decided against another. 'He'll be back by tomorrow.' He let the barman serve Kelly's drink then, as they were left on their own again, asked, 'Tell me, did Hayston know you'd sent Jane back to the cottage for that stopwatch?'

'Not till she'd been.' Kelly winced a little at the memory. 'And when he heard he pretty nearly hit the roof for some reason, but don't ask me why.' He looked beyond Thane as the door squeaked open again. A group of guests wandered in, then Kelly gave a nudge. 'We've got company.'

Stanley was in a lounge suit. By his side, Lynne Carter had her long, blonde hair brushed out so that it flowed down to her shoulders and lay like gold against her simple, expensively cut dark blue dress. They nodded towards Thane then drifted over to one of the tables. But, once Stanley had seen the blonde widow settled, he came back to the bar.

'Holding a wake?' he asked abruptly.

'Steady on, David,' protested Kelly, frowning.

'I don't feel much reason to,' said Stanley balefully. 'What about it, Thane? What's

206

happening — or do we sit around and wait to find out who's next on the list?'

'There's plenty being done, Mr Stanley.' Thane held the empty glass lightly between his fingertips. 'I've no miracles up my sleeve, but miracles don't solve murder.'

'That's what I mean.' Stanley scowled, a restless, impatient figure. 'Just when does it finish?'

'Don't you think we'd like to know?' Thane laid down the glass. 'Any reaction from your Ministry people about the test performances?'

'Uh-huh.' Stanley brightened a little. ''All systems go' so far. Tomorrow there's another session on the hill, some water-splashes, and a spot of road mileage — all easy after today. Friday's the real decider, the timed road climbs round Applecross and the Pass of Cattle. That's the finish — and I'll be damned glad when it comes.' He chewed briefly on a stray tendril of beard. 'Having two killings to worry about is enough to take the fire out of anyone's belly.'

'I've noticed two people who are reasonably happy,' murmured Kelly. 'Young Shaw and your secretary seem to be hitting it off.'

'I hadn't noticed.' Stanley showed his surprise. 'I'd class Jane Maulden in the icicle category — if he can thaw her out he's got talent.'

Thane took the chance. 'I haven't seen either of them around. Where are they?'

Stanley shrugged. 'Jane's boarding at a farmhouse down the road — accommodation's tight in this part of the world. Shaw's out at the hill with Danny Benson. They're doing a night watchman act on the test vehicles.'

'Was Shaw with you all morning?'

'Shaw — yes, I think so. Right, Bart?'

'Don't ask me,' complained Kelly. 'I was too busy running up and down that hill to notice anyone.'

'He wasn't far away.' Stanley's eyes narrowed. 'Something on your mind, Thane?'

'Just checking.'

'Then that's it — and I'd better get back,' declared Stanley, his interest flagging. 'Time I got Lynne a drink.'

'And I'm for bed,' decided Kelly, sliding from his stool. 'There's a 7 a.m. start tomorrow, and the hospital medic who strapped me up said I was to rest.'

Thane watched them go then, a moment later, rose in turn. How were things working out — that was what Stanley and the rest wanted to know, wanted to know for a variety of reasons. Well, at least he now had the beginnings of a belief, part of it pure hunch, part based on projecting possible fact to possible conclusion. At worst, it narrowed the field of his suspects. At best — no, it was too early to start on that, and there was little he could do till morning, till the technicians began reporting, till Phil Moss got back.

Except, of course, hoping that the pot wouldn't boil over again in the interim.

He ate a solitary meal in the hotel dining-room, their last cutomer of the evening. When he'd finished, he strolled back out into the hotel foyer, considered tele-phoning Headquarters, then hesitated. Dan Laurence adopted the old theatrical attitude of 'Don't call us, we'll call you' when his Bureau was at work.

Next moment, the decision was taken out of his hands.

'Hello, Thane.' Commander Allowes was standing by the entrance door, an old raincoat buttoned round his portly figure, a slight smile lighting his round, moon-like face. 'I was coming to look for you.'

'And you've found me.' Thane eyed him frostily.

'Fancy a walk?' The Admiralty man's expression changed, like the brief click of a camera shutter. 'I think it would be — well, beneficial.'

Thane nodded and, without a word, following him outside where the hotel lights formed a brief oasis before the start of the empty darkness of the hills. The wind had risen a little, sighing its way through the nearby trees, pushing heavy clouds across the black, star-crusted sky.

Allowes led the way, along a broad pathway then, more slowly, across the rough ground beyond until they reached a tumble-down dry-stone wall. He stopped, looked back the way they'd come, and sighed. 'Far enough, I'd say. I've done enough foot-slogging for one day.'

'It can get wearying,' agreed Thane with a hint of sarcasm.

The security man took it with a brief grimace. 'Thane, ever heard of a man called Koltsov — Alexis Koltsov? There was a poet of that name, early nineteenth century. I've read his stuff in the original, and he was pretty good.' He grimaced again. 'It's all right. I didn't bring you out to discuss poetry. The Koltsov I'm more interested in is — well, the official London Embassy title is 'cultural attaché.' Right now, if you inquired down there, they'd politely tell you he was on 'local leave.'' He stopped, his face a round, grey blob in the starlight, a blob with a suddenly thin, hard line of a mouth. 'He's spending it touring the North-West Highlands. In fact he's in a hotel less than twenty miles away.'

There was a tired intensity in his voice which gripped Thane's attention. There was, too, an invitation.

'I'd like to hear the rest,' said Thane slowly.

'You've been wondering what the devil I've been playing at,' mused Allowes, almost to himself. 'When I wandered off this afternoon I could feel my ears crisping. But — well, I told you earlier I was up here for reasons of my own. You had your job and I had mine. Now — let's say they're coming together, or should do pretty soon.'

'And I'm invited to join the party?' Thane couldn't help the distrust in the words.

'Something like that.' Allowes leaned back against the tumbledown wall. 'Koltsov is a travelling post office, we're pretty sure of it. He has full diplomatic immunity, this cultural jazz means he can wander where he wants and always say he's collecting old folk-songs or something equally weird. But on a time-cycle basis — ' he shrugged. 'Piecing it together, he's been too often around an area just about the time of a security leak — not that we've usually realised the leakage till later. Our guess is he's the man who collected the last batch of details from the Hydrostat Drives plant. On the same trip he probably collected another package of stuff on a metallurgical project.'

'I see.' Quietly, Thane took out his cigarettes and offered them. Allowes took one, cupped his hands round the flame of Thane's lighter and drew deeply.

'Thanks.' He treated the gesture as an unspoken understanding. 'Thane, take it that Koltsov's on a collection. Then ask yourself what he might be collecting.'

'More stuff from the Hydrostat plant is one pretty obvious answer.' Thane frowned, conscious of an uncertainty. 'He's making it pretty obvious, isn't he?'

'Maybe he has to, because he thinks his supply man is running out of time. I think Hayston was killed to make that time last a little longer.' Allowes smoked in silence for a moment. The high, sudden, death-scream of a rabbit came from somewhere on the hills, the scream as some marauder pounced. Thane felt the night air grow chill.

'How do I help?'

'If' — Allowes corrected himself sharply — 'when you discover your murderer, don't grab him straight off. I'm hoping he'll be the one Koltsov is waiting to meet.'

'He may have done it already.'

Allowes shook his head. 'Not yet. We've got him under a pretty tight surveillance. Anyway, if I were Koltsov I'd wait — and hope to earn a bonus by getting the result of these vehicle transmission tests. Now, what's your position?'

'Waiting and hoping.' Thane gave him a quick rundown on the situation.

'Then we've just got to be patient,' murmured Allowes. 'Incidentally — ' he stopped and grinned.

'Well?'

'Just a thought. If you'd like a close-up view of this Alexis Koltsov be out at the test slope tomorrow, about noon.'

'Eh?' Thane swallowed hard.

Allowes nodded. 'He's visiting us. I — ah — arranged the invitation. I thought it might prove interesting.' He dropped his cigarette, let it glow for a moment on the grass, then ground it underfoot. 'And now I think I'll go to bed. Good night, Thane.'

7

A brief forty minutes after take-off the evening flight from Inverness touched down at Glasgow, and by six-thirty Phil Moss arrived by taxi at Headquarters.

It was the quiet time in the big building in St Andrews Street. The administration offices were closed, the bulk of the night teams were out on the start of their particular prowls, and the first arrests were still in transit. Later it would be different — as the divisions began their nightly requests for assistance, as the pubs closed, and the neds began making mischief, as the professionals set to work. But for the moment the place had all the peace of a well-ordered public library — down to a party of Church Guild members being shown the sights of the Black Museum's weapon collection up on the second floor.

Moss delivered his package of bomb fragments to the duty man in the Scientific Bureau front office, promised to look back later, then made his way to the Central C.I.D. muster room. The shift inspector was Pete Franklin, a University honours graduate who one day would probably make Chief Constable — but for the moment he was just another overworked cop with a long night stretching ahead.

'I heard you were coming.' Franklin scratched around his desk and found an old envelope he was using as a message pad. 'This is yours, Phil — Inland Revenue, Glasgow Region Headquarters, St Vincent Street, seven o'clock. You've to see a Mr Carlson. Okay?'

Moss grunted and scribbled the details on a page of his notebook. 'Anything else?'

Franklin shrugged. 'Not here, mate — that's all I've got.' He eyed Moss hopefully. 'How about looking in again later, and we could maybe nip out for a quick jar? I could use a nice, cool beer.'

The invitation was hard to resist. Moss sucked his teeth reflectively. 'Well, I could, if — '

'If what?' Franklin sensed a catch.

'If one of your boys runs a check for me beforehand.'

Franklin sighed, found a spare corner of the envelope and looked up. 'Let's have it.'

'I want to be sure that a couple who called themselves Mr and Mrs David Stanley spent Sunday night at the place they claim — when they arrived, whether either of them left at any time.'

'Going into the divorce business, Phil?' Franklin grinned, then listened and wrote while Moss gave details and descriptions. 'All right, I'll see it's done. But you'd better get moving — those Inland Revenue characters don't like being kept waiting.'

Mr Arnold Carlson, one of Her Majesty's inspectors of taxes and deputy principal, Glasgow area, said much the same thing but in greater detail some fifteen minutes later when Moss finally penetrated to that Civil Servant's inner sanctum, an office on the top floor of the high, modern block dedicated to the pursuit of the city's taxpayers.

'We're happy to co-operate, but we do usually keep to normal — ah — business hours,' said Carlson, a large, ruddy-faced individual who, despite his stiff white collar and dark lounge suit looked as though he'd be more at home on a golf course than sitting behind his ultra-modern steel desk. 'Still, from what Chief Inspector Thane told me by telephone the circumstances are unusual. Some of my staff have agreed to work late, and I cancelled a social engagement of my own.'

Moss muttered appropriate thanks and perched uneasily on the edge of his chair. Tax offices worried him, brought back memories of the two years he'd forgotten to declare his savings account interest as income. Somehow they'd never challenged the gap.

'Eh — we're certainly hoping you can help us, Mr Carlson,' he said, noting the desk bare of all except an unmarked blotting pad and a water carafe, the way in which the small telephone and intercom table to one side had the directories on its lower shelf arranged in military precision. 'Your records may be able to fill some of the gaps we're up against.'

'I'm certain of it!' Carlson gave a satisfied smile. 'In fact, I'm surprised you people don't turn up here more often.'

'We don't usually need — '

Carlson shook his head. 'You don't usually appreciate, I'd say. Tax assessment isn't just income detail, it's a complete picture of a person's way of life, revised annually. Dependent relatives, marital status, children, employment history, investments, insurances, bank interest, rent paid or house loan interest, whether you use a car for work, business expenses, union subscriptions — it's rather like the marriage vow, Inspector. We're with everyone in sickness and in health, for richer or for poorer — '

'Till death you do part?'

'Well, we're still interested in estate duty,' mused Carlson. 'We make sure you don't take it with you — at least, not until tax has been assessed at the appropriate rate.' He laughed at his own joke, then swivelled round in his chair and flicked one of the intercom switches. 'Mr Delby . . . '

The disembodied Delby's voice replied after the briefest of intervals. 'Sir?'

'Our police inquiry — William Carter and others.' Carlson beamed briefly towards Moss. 'How far have we got?'

'We're working from his file now, sir,' reported the voice crisply. 'There's an interesting underpayment in 1960 I noticed — '

'Later,' interrupted Carlson impatiently. 'What about the rest?'

'His last return before reclassification as self-employed was five years ago, when he was with a firm Tipland Engineering. The man Peter Hayston was also employed there, but left Tipland on the same tax-week. There's no Maulden listed on the firm's wage return for that year, but we do have a rebate claim in that name, we're working from there.'

'And this fourth man — ah — ' Carlson frowned towards Moss.

'Shaw.'

'Yes, what about Shaw?' demanded Carlson.

'There's an Ian Shaw on the closed file master list,' reported the invisible Delby. 'That takes longer, sir — these emigrant cases are always a problem. I sent you a memo about re-filing and — '

'Later.' Carlson closed the switch and sighed. 'Well, we're making some progress. But we'll need a little more time, I'm afraid.'

'I'd say you've got off to a good start,' declared Moss, considerably impressed.

'Cradle to the grave, part of the job,' declared Carlson modestly. 'Of course, there can be gaps in the case of casual workers, but we've always some reference to insurance, unemployment benefit or the like, even if their records are — er — not quite so well organised.' He stroked his upper lip thoughtfully. 'Still, it would help us if you knew of any special feature about any of these men.'

Moss shrugged. 'We know Maulden's a permanent invalid, in a nursing home in Edinburgh.'

'He has relatives?'

'There's a daughter, Jane. She's a secretary with Hydrostat Drives.'

'Ah!' Carlson was satisfied. 'Then she should be claiming a dependent relative allowance. That makes it much easier. And don't worry about this fellow Shaw. Emigration cases are withdrawn from our files after a period, but their tax histories are still kept in a separate records section. You never can tell when they could be needed.' He glanced at his watch. 'Still, I'm afraid we may not have a complete picture before morning, Inspector. Supposing we leave it till 9 a.m. — would that do? Delby can take things so far tonight, then I'll have him come in early tomorrow — '

Moss found himself being shepherded towards the door. 'I'll be here first thing,' he promised.

'Settled, then.' Polite but impatient, Carlson had the door open. 'Come any time — oh, and if you've any personal taxation problems we'll be happy to advise. I could have your file looked out, and — '

Moss declined the offer, mumbled his thanks, and beat a hasty retreat.

★　★　★

The city's pulse was quickening as night wore on. By the time he'd had a quick meal in the Headquarters canteen the building housed a steadily increasing bustle of activity. Up in the Scientific Bureau area, he waited patiently at the night counter while the duty sergeant issued a Northern Division man receipts for a butcher's hook and a blood-stained shirt, both brought in from a street battle.

The sergeant finished the job, dumped the productions in separate boxes, then greeted him with a nod. 'The boss is handling yours, Inspector — like to go through?'

He found Dan Laurence at one of the work benches in the main laboratory area. The Bureau chief's stained white overall coat was hanging loose and a cigarette smouldered on the edge of the crowded bench.

''Evening, Phil.' Laurence knocked the ash from his cigarette and put it back in his mouth. 'Well, I hope you're not expecting great things — there's not a hell o' a lot to tell you about this stuff.' He thumbed towards the bomb fragments, piled neatly to one side. 'Quite nice wee jobs, both of them.'

'That's nice to know,' growled Moss. 'I'd hate to be blown up by an amateur.'

Laurence grinned and scratched his head with the tip of a fine-bladed screwdriver. 'Aye, it's undignified. Well, it was plastic explosive, the usual terrorist-sabotage variety. The casings were just a couple o' old bits of iron piping, plugged at the ends. He used acid-tube pencil fuses — that's what gave the few seconds delay. Activation was by contact release.' He moved the screwdriver's attentions to under his chin. 'Aye, you were lucky to walk out of it.'

'How long would it take to rig the things?'

'Five minutes each for assembly, just a moment or two to place them. And he could carry that plastic goo around in anything from a toothpaste tube upwards. It could be inside a car tyre, anywhere.'

Moss nodded. It was stuff which could be moulded, hammered, even burned in a fire — only when a detonator was attached did it become lethal.

'That's the lot as far as the bombs are concerned. Let's see now — ' Laurence ran his eye along the bench then pounced on a pair of large household scissors. 'These next. Colin asked for a check on Hayston's flat. We did it, an' found a reasonable collection of photogear — nothing fancy, an ordinary hobby layout. No pictures or negatives lyin' around that meant anything, but we took these scissors. The blade edges match the cuttin' pattern on the edge o' that picture everybody's pulling Colin's leg about.'

Moss took the scissors and idly checked the blades. 'Dan, could Hayston have done a copying job?'

'Only a botched one,' declared Laurence emphatically. 'His gear was happy snaps stuff, not spy category.' He dismissed the idea from his mind. 'While you're here, there are a couple o' other things worth knowing. The time-lock movement we lifted is the same as one that turned up in one of our embassies over there a while back. And I've a message lying somewhere from Army records. David Stanley is blood group O, which lets him out.'

Neither was a particular surprise. Moss thanked him, left, and headed over to the Central C.I.D. room.

Pete Franklin greeted him like a lost brother and glanced quickly at the clock on the wall. 'We've still time for that jar, Phil — and it's on me. You deserve it.'

'Eh?' Moss raised an eyebrow. 'What's happened? If it's the hotel enquiry — '

'That?' Franklin shook his head. 'Their story checks. Arrived about seven on the Sunday evening, didn't leave until around eight the next morning.'

'Then — ' Moss showed his bewilderment.

'You saw the Regional Squad yesterday and mentioned you were interested in a character named Clark, right?'

'Yes, but — ' Moss swallowed.

'We've got him in a cell through the back,' said Pete Franklin happily. 'He was picked up about an hour ago.'

'What charge?'

Franklin gave him an old-fashioned look. 'Counterfeit notes — come off it, Phil. The Regional boys checked through their general circulation reports, and came up with an advice message from Brighton police — all they had was that a middle-aged woman, probably a Scot by her accent, had passed dud notes in half a dozen shops in town.'

Moss groaned aloud. 'Then what?'

'They contacted Brighton, who found Splits Clark had been registered under his own name at a hotel in town while this woman was operating. The hotel staff tipped them he'd been going around most of the time with another of their guests. Her name's — '

'Emma Robertson.' Moss closed his eyes for a second, dreading the rest.

'So you had that up your sleeve, too!' Franklin thumped his desk in delight, oblivious to his companion's despair. 'Well, they passed the case over to us for action this evening. We've got them both.'

'Pete — ' Moss drew a deep breath. 'Emma Robertson happens to be my landlady. Where is she?'

'In a cell, but — ' Franklin's mouth dropped open. 'If she's your landlady, what the heck's this all about?'

'Clark had her hooked for a wedding service,' grated Moss. 'If she passed any notes you can be sure he gave her them — but that she'd no idea they were phoney.'

'Brighton say they were first-class forgeries,' admitted Franklin, now looking far from happy. 'Look, Phil, she didn't mention she knew you.'

'What does she say about the notes?'

Franklin grimaced. 'So far all she's told us is that she'll sue every cop in the city. Phil, I'm sorry about this. But we nailed Clark cold, found a briefcase filled with counterfeit stuff under a floorboard in his room. He's not talking, but it seemed cast-iron they were in it together.'

'Have you charged her yet?'

'No, she's still just detained for questioning.' Franklin was silent for some seconds, trying to make up his mind. 'Phil, if you're sure — '

'Positive.'

'Well, we could try to get a statement out of her, then let her go until this is sorted out.' He brightened and gave a quick snap of his fingers. 'You could go through now and explain it to her!'

'Me?' Moss paled at the thought. 'I want nothing to do with it.'

'All right.' Franklin gave a wry grin. 'I'll sort it out, no names. Then you can buy me that drink.'

Moss agreed willingly. But he had another

problem. 'If she's going home, where do I spend the night?'

'Scared to face her?'

'Terrified,' admitted Moss.

'Well . . . ' Franklin thought for a moment. 'There's an old couch along in the spare interview room, if you're interested.'

It didn't matter much. Phil Moss had a feeling he wasn't going to find it easy getting to sleep.

★   ★   ★

Colin Thane slept soundly until 7 a.m. then groaned awake, cursing the noise and sounds of bustle coming from the hotel courtyard. The Hydrostat convoy was leaving on schedule, but he wished they could have achieved it in smoother style. He lay where he was, listening to the revving engines, the shouts, the slamming of doors, and, at last, the sound of vehicles pulling away. Then, as the final engine faded, he turned on his side for a few more moments.

When he next wakened and glanced at his watch it was after eight. He yawned his way out of bed, drew open the curtains, and looked out. The weather had changed for the worse. Grey clouds hid the mountain tops, dulling the greens and browns of their lower slopes. The wind was coming from the north-west, bringing more than a hint of rain in its wake. Thane turned back, lit a cigarette, and coughed his way through the first few puffs before starting to dress.

Half an hour later, washed and shaved, he strolled down to the dining-room. A scattering of guests were still at breakfast, and the glum-faced waiter guided him over to share a table. The other occupant was the tweed-suited man he'd seen in the bar the night before, the Glenpeak Arms' hill-walker. Early rising and galloping up and down mountains obviously created their own appetite. Anderson was tackling a plate of bacon and eggs with steam-shovel enthusiasm.

Thane took the seat opposite, ordered toast and coffee, and stifled another yawn.

'Aye, I feel that way sometimes myself,' said the other man, eyeing him with mild amusement. 'A late night, eh?'

'Sometimes wonder if there's another kind,' confessed Thane.

'The name's Anderson, Ronald Anderson,' volunteered the hill-walker. 'Eh — and in a place like this it's not hard to identify new arrivals. I heard about yesterday's explosion, Chief Inspector.'

Thane nodded. His order arrived a moment later, and he poured himself a cup of coffee then glanced thoughtfully across the table. 'From what I was told in the bar last night you spend a lot of time in the hills.'

'Three weeks every year,' Anderson said happily. 'The other forty-nine I work in a bank. But this is my holiday — and my hobby. Naturalist, botanist — the labels don't really fit. I just like walking in the high places, by myself, plodding around.'

Thane nodded towards the dining-room window. 'But not in this weather, I'd imagine.'

Anderson shrugged. 'I've been up one of the glens for a couple of hours. Some of the deer were down fairly low, feeding — I had my glasses on them for a spell.' He chuckled. 'The more I see of people at the bank, the more I'm inclined to prefer animals.'

'I know that feeling.' Thane buttered some toast then glanced speculatively at the man. 'Any outside chance that you had those glasses on the cottage yesterday morning?'

'Sorry.' Anderson shook his head. 'I was over in that direction, but quite a distance away.' His meal finished, he lit a cigarette. 'Mind you, there was someone else out on the hills yesterday, and fairly near the place. If you found him maybe he could help.'

'You saw somebody?' Thane quietly laid down his cup and leaned forward. 'When?'

'A little after eleven.' Anderson showed embarrassment at the interest he'd aroused. 'I can't really tell you much more than that, Chief Inspector. I just noticed a man walking on the hill above the cottage, perhaps a mile away. There are some quite rare Alpine plants on that hillside — probably he was out collecting.'

The time fitted. Jane Maulden would have been back at the test slope for more than half an hour by then. Thane knew a sudden, unreasoning elation. 'Could he have come from the cottage?'

'He could have come from anywhere, I suppose.' Anderson shrugged. 'But, seriously now — '

'I'm being very serious, Mr Anderson,' said Thane bluntly. 'Where was he heading?'

'West, over the shoulder of the hill — '

'In the direction of the Ministry test slope?'

'I've never been there but — yes, I suppose one could reach it that way. There's no path, of course.'

'Describe him.'

'On a casual glance, through glasses, and at least a mile between us?' Anderson was dazed at the thought. 'Well, he was bare-headed, and — ' he stopped, shaking his head. 'You couldn't call this evidence, Chief Inspector.'

'I didn't.' Thane waited, his whole manner

hard and demanding.

Anderson frowned unhappily. 'I don't think he was a young man. A young man on a hill is inclined to travel in a straight line, whatever the obstacles. This fellow — well, he moved confidently, he'd stamina. But he took the easy ways. They're usually quicker at the end of the day. That's something animals know by instinct from birth, but we've got to learn by experience.' He took a deep breath. 'I'm sorry, but that's all, positively all I can tell you.'

'It's enough.' Thane relaxed. 'Thanks, Mr Anderson.'

Anderson cleared his throat a couple of times, got no encouragement to ask the questions on his mind, and finally rose, gave a puzzled nod, and left.

Once he'd gone, Thane sat back with a sigh. At last he felt reason to justify the nagging suspicion that had been with him for so long, the vague possibility that two separate sets of events might have collided through chance then been manipulated until they reacted as one on the people concerned.

But if that had happened it created its own bleak suspicion, with only one way to probe towards the truth — whether the answer that waited was one he expected or not.

The hall porter paged him to take a

telephone call at exactly nine. Thane went to the private booth in the hotel foyer, heard Moss's voice grate peevishly from the receiver, and greeted him cheerfully.

'What luck so far, Phil?'

'I've got troubles but they'll keep,' said Moss gloomily. 'The rest is fine. Inland Revenue have it all tied up, and I'm at the airport now, ready to leave.'

'Maulden and Shaw fit in?'

'Completely,' confirmed Moss. 'And it looks like Hayston took that pretty picture of you on Monday night. Want the details?'

'No, they'll keep till you get here,' Thane assured him. 'What else have you got?'

'Stanley's hotel story checks out and his blood group is the wrong shade,' reported Moss sourly. 'And I've got Professor Mac-Master as a fellow passenger. I'd have thought the old vulture could have flapped up on his own.'

Thane grinned but was unsympathetic. 'Sergeant Kingsley will collect you at Inverness — I'll expect you here about two this afternoon. How long till your flight's called, Phil?'

'Ten, fifteen minutes.' His second-in-command was instantly suspicious. 'Why?'

'It gives you time enough to line up something.' The words came down the line with a familiar, almost lazy emphasis, one Moss knew well, a clear signal that Colin Thane had at last decided his course. 'Phil, get our own lads at Division to handle this — no channelling through Donfoot or Headquarters. They've to get a list of all the firms who use Bart Kelly as their public relations man. After that, I want to know if our Commander Allowes really was in London all the weekend . . . and how long he's been stationed in the Clyde area. They're to get the answers to me as soon as they can.'

Moss whistled softly. 'But Kelly — '

'Saved your life and probably mine, I know.'

'And if Allowes gets to hear of this — '

'Then it could be awkward,' admitted Thane. 'That's why I want our own lads handling it.'

He hung up. One more task remained, one he'd deliberately held back on till now. The reception desk gave him directions to the farmhouse where Jane Maulden was being boarded out, and when a county patrol car arrived, ready to run him over to the test slope, he had the uniformed driver make the detour.

The farmhouse was big and old fashioned, the farmer's wife was built to match, and it took a lot of persuasion before she'd let him see Jane Maulden's room. But after that it didn't take long — it never did, when you were a cop and had done the same job so many times before.

The bed and wardrobe yielded nothing, and he heard the farmer's wife, watching suspiciously from the doorway, sniff indignantly as he turned to the heavy oak dressing table and remove its drawers one by one. The drawers held only a few items of clothing, and he ignored them. But when the last one had been dumped on the floor he reached into the dark space at the rear of the dressing table. His fingers brushed then gripped on a small package, and a moment later he had William Carter's desk diary.

'Is that what you wanted — just that?' asked the farmer's wife.

Thane nodded and glanced quickly through its pages. The space for the Sunday on which Carter had died had only one entry — 'Shaw, 1 p.m.' He slipped the diary into his pocket, put the drawers back into the dressing table, then thanked the woman and left.

The county car delivered him to the foot of the test slope by 11 a.m. As it drove off again he looked around, shivering a little in the cold wind and a steady drizzle of rain.

The Hydrostat car was going through its paces and, though the rain might be holding down the dust of the previous day it was in turn creating a fresh difficulty, turning the loose, gravel-like surface into a slippery, treacherous course. A gruff voice cursed close at hand as the grey saloon's tail began sliding at one of the taped bends, its wheels spinning for grip.

Thane turned and saw Danny Benson following the vehicle's progress with tight-lipped concentration, hands deep in the pockets of his greasy overalls.

'Worried, Danny?' he asked.

'A bit, Mr Thane,' confessed the elderly mechanic. 'Ach, if it was Mr Stanley behind that wheel I'd feel happier. But young Shaw's takin' the drive. The lad's good but he hasn't the same touch — an' look what those Ministry bods have done.'

The Ministry men had taken advantage of conditions. The white tapes had been altered, changed to a layout of erratic curves and loops, some with tight bends, others with stop and start lines placed on the worst sections of the loose surface. Thane's driving instinct winced as the car above hit another of those loose patches, engine racing, stones spattering machine-gun style from beneath the whirling tyres.

'We'll just need to keep hopin',' said Benson gloomily. 'Sometimes it comes down to luck, Mr Thane. Either you have it or you don't. I remember a car I crewed from first prototype through to the day we put on a special pre-release show for a bunch o' motoring writers. Not a bit o' trouble till then — but that was the day the thing caught fire an' burned out. Just luck, that's all.'

Thane chuckled. 'These things happen.'

'Aye.' Benson's attention was back with the car and its driver. As far as he was concerned, Thane no longer existed.

After a moment, Thane moved on, threading his way through the motley collection of vehicles. A space had been left at one point, and a uniformed constable prowled nearby, ready to defend it against all comers. The man saw him, stiffened a little, then relaxed again at Thane's easy nod.

'When's your V.I.P. due?' asked Thane.

'On his way now, sir.' The man thumbed up the slope. 'This looks like the reception committee getting ready.'

One of the Ministry vehicles, a Land-Rover, was crawling down the access track from the top of the slope. It bounced towards them, stopped, and Commander Allowes climbed out, followed by David Stanley and Lynne Carter.

'You timed it nicely, Thane,' said the little security man, padding over and greeting him

235

warmly. 'Koltsov's being punctual.' He made sure the others were out of earshot, and asked quietly, 'Any progress?'

'A lot,' said Thane shortly. 'Once Phil Moss arrives I'd like you to be handy.'

'I'll make a point of it,' declared Allowes, nodding fractionally. 'Just remember the one thing I'm asking. Don't grab your man straight off. Give things time to — well, mature.'

'We will,' promised Thane dryly.

On the test slope, the car had found easier going. It finished the last stage in a burst of smooth acceleration and came to a halt at the finish line. Allowes paid scant attention. A long black limousine was purring towards the vehicle park from the roadway. A Russian Zis, with prominent C.D. plates, it swung into the reserved space, stopped, and a chauffeur nipped out to open the rear doors.

'No flag up front,' murmured Allowes. 'Protocol — this is only a semi-official visit. Embassy chauffeur, of course.' He continued his commentary as the three passengers alighted. 'The one with the broad shoulders is a secretary-interpreter — though Koltsov can speak English as well as you or I. The tall one, like a bean-pole and with no chin, is a Civil Servant, one of the Scottish Office permanent under-somethings laid on to spread sweetness

236

and light during the trip. There's Koltsov now.'

Alexis Koltsov, cultural attaché and travelling postman, was a slim, sallow man of medium height, with dark hair just beginning to grey at the temples, a small mouth and dark, bright eyes. He wore a brown sports coat over a high necked grey wool jersey and well-cut slacks, his shoes were immaculately polished, and he seemed briskly interested in all that was going on around him.

Allowes' left eyelid dropped in a quick wink. 'Here I go, Thane.'

'You?'

'Why not?' grinned Allowes. 'If he's even semi-efficient he knows I'm here and why, so what's the odds?'

The security man bustled across, spoke briefly to the Scottish Office guide, then turned to shake Koltsov warmly by the hand. A moment later he was introducing Lynne Carter and Stanley to their guest. Koltsov reacted to the blonde's presence with a heel-clicking smile and stopped just short of a comrade-style embrace, then began talking in animated fashion. Thane watched it all with a slight sense of unreality, a glimpse of a world of fragile, politely preserved fictions.

The preliminaries over, Koltsov was quickly shepherded across to the Land-Rover and climbed aboard, his hosts following. Thane glanced back at the Zis, then his unconscious scowl changed to a twist of a smile. The uniformed constable was offering Koltsov's chauffeur a cigarette and the secretary-interpreter's attention was being taken up by a man whose mechanic's overalls were just a shade too clean to be genuine. Protocol might be one thing — but the game, it seemed, was well organised.

The visit lasted a little more than an hour while the light, misting rain continued and the clouds crept lower. Koltsov and his party inspected the vehicles, examined the slope's taped layout, then saw the car and truck go through their paces one after the other. Halfway through, still waiting by the start line, Thane felt a nudge against his ribs.

'My old mother would say this was enough to make a saint spin in his grave,' murmured Bart Kelly, inclining his head towards the distant guest group. 'Hell, I know there's no security risk involved, but it doesn't seem decent. They're doin' everything except give him one in a present.'

'It's called diplomacy,' grunted Thane.

'Is it now?' Kelly raised a caustic eyebrow. 'What do they call leavin' booby-trap bombs around?'

'We don't know they did,' corrected Thane.

'Who else would?' Kelly rubbed one hand irately over his close-cut grey hair. 'This damned damp is getting into my bones and I still feel like somebody used me for a football. Hell, I'm a taxpayer and I object.'

'Allowes would tell you to be as objectionable as you like, but to do it somewhere else.'

Kelly swore bitterly and wandered off.

The visit ended in high style — Koltsov's party being ferried down the slope in the Hydrostat truck, a final series of salutations as they climbed back into the big black Zis, then Allowes and David Stanley giving a last wave as the car purred off the way it had come.

'And that's that!' Allowes permitted himself a rare amount of emotion, took out a large white handkerchief, and used it to mop the moisture from his forehead. He looked around and grinned. 'Thanks, everybody. The Cultural Attaché was most impressed.'

'So let's get back to work,' growled David Stanley. 'The circus is over. Danny — ' he beckoned the mechanic forward. 'We've got to give them some reduced power timings on the truck. You know what to do?'

Danny Benson nodded. 'Who's drivin'?'

Stanley chewed his beard for a moment. Ian Shaw stood nearby, an expectant look on his face. But the Hydrostat chief shook his head. 'I'll take it this time. Come on, let's move.'

The men around got to work. Ian Shaw hesitated, then was moving to join them when Stanley called him over.

'You're doing fine, Ian. But I'd rather take this next bit on my own — and know you're keeping an eye on the preparation side.'

'Fair enough.' The young red-head smiled lazily towards Thane. 'Like me to find you a job, Chief Inspector?'

'I'm happy as things are,' said Thane mildly.

'Gossip later,' said Stanley curtly. 'And Ian, try not to rub Danny the wrong way — you're the transmission man, but the vehicles are still his personal babies.'

Shaw grinned and went on his way.

Hands on his hips, Stanley was impatient to get under way. 'I thought they'd pull this one on us,' he said, his voice a blend of grim satisfaction. 'The better things go, the tougher these Ministry men become.'

'What's next?' asked Thane, watching the bustle of activity round the truck.

'Simulation stuff. They want us to operate on three-wheel then two-wheel drive, as if we'd had pipe failures. I've told them it wouldn't happen, but — ' Stanley's heavy-shoulderd shrug summed up his opinion of the whole affair.

The drizzle of rain had died away by the time the reduced power runs were finished. Stanley brought the truck coasting back from the finish line, switched off the engine, and declared a lunch break.

'But nobody disappears,' he warned. 'Another hour here, then we pack up and move across to the Pass of Cattle location. I want everything organised for a clean start tomorrow.'

For the first time since he'd arrived, Thane saw Jane Maulden. The dark-haired girl was presiding over a table laden with hampers. Lynne Carter beside her, both busy issuing packed sandwiches and coffee flasks to the queue which formed around them. When Shaw's turn came, the girl talked to him briefly, laughed at something he said, then turned to serve her next customer. Thane joined the queue's tail, drew a strained smile from Lynne Carter as she served him, then walked quietly off on his own.

The lunch-break had ended and the slope was busy again when Phil Moss arrived two minutes before 2 p.m. He eased himself wearily from Sergeant Kingsley's car and brightened when he saw Thane waiting.

'This is yours — ' he produced a thick

envelope and handed it over. 'Any word from the Division?'

Thane shook his head, opened the envelope, and gave all his attention to the Inland Revenue report. At last he refolded the papers, whistling faintly between his teeth. 'Right, Phil, let's get on with it. We'll use the cottage kitchen — I'll collect Allowes, you get the girl. Better tell Stanley he'll be without a secretary for the rest of the afternoon, and that if anyone asks where she's gone he's packed her off on some errand.'

'One thing first.' Moss's thin face twisted with unhappy embarrassment. 'Colin, old MacMaster wants to see you soon as you're through. And he gave me a message for you, such as it is. He says that if Carter was in any sort of a fight on Sunday, it was a good few hours before he died — eight or more.'

'What makes him so certain?'

'I don't know,' confessed Moss. 'He just threw it at me out of the blue — says he'll explain it when he sees you.'

Thane swore impatiently. 'So he can have an audience for a lecture?' But the message was welcome, particularly because it dovetailed neatly with his own idea of events that Sunday.

* * *

Commander Allowes was ready and willing, Jane Maulden reluctant but resigned. Sergeant Kingsley had driven them to the cottage — all but the Commander, who used his red Mercedes in a gesture of independence. The local constable was still mounting guard outside the damaged building and, as Kingsley drove off again, Thane left the uniformed man on watch outside and led the others through to the kitchen. As they entered, he stood by the doorway, his face impassive.

After waiting a moment, Jane Maulden pursed her lips, deliberately scraped a chair towards the table, and sat down. 'Well, Mr Thane?'

'Another talk, Jane,' he told her. 'Inspector Moss spent most of the night working with tax inspectors back in Glasgow. They were digging into their records — can you guess what they found?'

She flickered a glance towards Moss, leaning against the kitchen stove, but shook her head.

'Carter, Hayston, your father and Ian Shaw all worked for the same firm a few years back, when you were still at school. You knew that, didn't you?'

She gnawed her lip for a moment, her face suddenly pale, then nodded.

Thane saw the surprise on Allowes' face, gave him a fractional smile, and pressed on in the same calm, demanding voice. 'Ian Shaw went to Canada when he was still an apprentice — and you didn't know him then, did you?'

This time, she gave a brief shake of her head.

'Lost your tongue, Jane?' queried Thane. 'Let's see if the rest is right. About a year after Shaw emigrated your father was injured in a road crash, crippled for life. A little later, William Carter branches out in business on his own after scraping together every penny he can — and strangely enough, Peter Hayston, no great brain, goes along with him.' He leaned forward, and tossed Carter's slim, leather-bound desk diary on the table in front of her. 'You know where this was, don't you?'

'I — ' she swallowed hard, and then tried to speak.

Thane cut her short. 'You know what's entered for Sunday, Jane. So let's have the truth, from the top down.'

'Hold on, Thane,' protested Allowes. 'I'm lost.'

'Ian Shaw was due to meet Carter at the plant at 1 p.m. on Sunday,' said Thane grimly. He swung back to the girl. 'You got that diary from this cottage, from Hayston's room, didn't you?'

'Yes, but — but I didn't — '

'Leave any bombs around?' Thane shrugged. 'Why not help us believe you?'

The three men waited silently. She shut her eyes for a moment then took a deep, sighing breath and looked up. 'All right. Do — do you want to caution me first or anything?'

Phil Moss fought back a grin. 'We'll worry about that when it's necessary, lassie,' he said gruffly. 'Just get on with it.'

She drew herself a little more upright in the chair. 'It starts with my father, then. That crash, Mr Thane — it was a bad one. The man who was driving was killed.'

'I see.' Thane produced the photograph he'd found in Hayston's wallet. 'Is he the other man in this picture?'

The girl glanced and nodded. 'Yes — he was a Mr Yarrow. I knew him and — well, maybe he was lucky. My father had head and spinal injuries when they found him, and the doctors couldn't do much.' She forced herself on. 'He lies in bed, sometimes sits in a chair, but he has no — no control, no mind or memory. It's — I suppose you could say he's like a vegetable, except that I sometimes think he knows who I am.'

Commander Allowes cleared his throat in

awkward fashion. 'How old were you when it happened?'

'Sixteen. My mother and I went to live in Edinburgh, to be near the nursing home — it's difficult to find a place that takes on his kind of case. My mother died about two years ago.' She bit her lip. 'That's when Mr Carter offered me this job. He'd visited the nursing home every other month and — well, he seemed to want to help. That's how it looked, anyway.'

'You've other ideas now?' asked Thane quietly.

'Yes.' She drew a deep breath. 'He must have wanted to keep an eye on me, Chief Inspector. These techniques that have won the firm orders — the marine equipment, the new vehicle transmission, the other things he's supposed to have developed — they're all based on work my father did.'

Thane's face didn't change. Once, earlier, what the girl was saying might have surprised him. But now it seemed almost reasonable, to be expected, part of a chain he could almost predict.

'Shaw told you this?'

'On Tuesday night, once we'd arrived here.' She flushed at the memory. 'I lost my temper over something he said about Carter. Then — well, he told me what he knew.' She gave a bitter little smile. 'When he'd finished, I was the one who apologised. Ian did come over for a holiday. But he also wanted to visit Hydrostat Drives, because he'd read about their work in some Canadian engineering journal and thought my father must be connected with the firm — felt he had to be, because of the valve gear techniques they were using.'

Moss scratched his thin thatch of hair and frowned. 'How could he be so sure?'

The girl shrugged. 'He was only an apprentice when he worked beside my father — but apprentices have time on their hands. Ian used to hang around him at tea-breaks and every lunch-hour — that was when he would work on the plan drawings and models.' She gave a slow, essentially sad smile. 'Ian says my father wouldn't touch them during actual working times — he didn't want to give the firm any claim on them.'

'But your father must have kept some of this stuff at home,' protested Allowes, puzzled. 'And there's such a thing as patent protection.'

'Only if you apply for it,' she said dully. 'And — well, it didn't mean anything till now. But I can remember Carter coming to our house soon after we knew my father wouldn't recover. He said the firm needed some drawings my father had been working on — and he took them.'

Thane considered her for a moment. 'Jane, what makes you so sure all this is true?'

'Because — because Ian told me he saw Carter at the plant on Sunday. But he didn't kill him.'

'Go on.'

She shook her head. 'That's up to Ian. Except — I'll tell you why he stayed over here, what he was doing. He challenged Carter, told him he could prove he'd stolen my father's work, and that he'd do it unless — '

'Unless Carter paid up?'

'To my father and to me.' She gave that twisted little smile again. 'And he's quite frank that he wanted some money for himself.'

'You could call it blackmail,' said Thane softly.

'I wouldn't.'

Thane walked slowly towards the window, looked out at the grey hills, then spun round on his heel. 'Shaw's appointment with Carter was for 1 p.m. on Sunday. After that we know he was through on the east coast, gawking at the Forth Road Bridge, about five in the evening. You say he didn't kill Carter. All right, help us prove he didn't — where else did he go that afternoon?'

'Before that?' She saw him nod. 'He was at the nursing home, visiting my father. It should be easy enough to check — when I got there the sister on duty told me a man had looked in earlier, though he hadn't left his name. I didn't know who it could have been at the time.'

'When did you arrive?'

'About four o'clock.'

Thane grinned. 'If that's the truth then it's all we need. Except . . . Jane, why did you look in Hayston's room for the desk diary?'

'Ian knew he had it.' She wouldn't say more.

'Where did you find it?'

'Hidden at the back of his dressing table — the same way I hid it in mine.'

Allowes took a long, sighing breath. 'Girl, you — ' he stopped and shook his head. 'Well, Thane, what now?'

'We have a long talk with Shaw and hope he's got sense enough to give us the rest. But it sounds like Hayston was kept on the payroll because he knew all about Carter's plundering.'

Jane Maulden rose to her feet. 'Can I go now?'

'No — not till I've seen Shaw,' Thane told

her. 'Anyway, the test team will have left the hill by now. They'll be making the move to tomorrow's location.' He pondered for a moment. 'Suppose I arrange for the local constable's wife to let you stay with her till we're ready — will you do it?'

She nodded quietly.

'Jane' — Phil Moss's curiosity got the better of him — 'why didn't you burn that desk diary?'

The question made her blink and search for an answer. 'I nearly did,' she admitted at last. 'But — well, it wouldn't have been right, would it?'

Even Moss couldn't think of a better answer.

★   ★   ★

Colin Thane took her outside, arranged matters with the local cop, and waited until the man had driven off, the girl settled back in the passenger seat of his small patrol van. When he went back into the kitchen he found Phil Moss and Commander Allowes still standing where he'd left them, Moss chewing a bismuth tablet, Allowes with a face which was an expressionless mask.

'Like to explain to me that business about how important it was to know when Shaw got to Edinburgh?' queried Allowes in vaguely annoyed fashion. 'I thought there was no fixed time of death.'

'I've to find out more about it myself,' said Thane almost curtly. 'All I've got so far is a message from MacMaster — and I'd like to know more myself.'

'And Shaw?'

'He'll keep.' Thane stopped and frowned as he heard the sound of a car approaching the cottage clearing. It stopped outside, they heard someone get out, and a few seconds later Detective Sergeant Kingsley ambled into the room.

'You're still here, eh?' The county man beamed around him. 'Where's the girl, sir?'

'Gone,' said Thane impatiently. 'Something wrong at the test slope, Sergeant?'

'No, they were moving off when I left and everything's fine.' Kingsley fished in his coat pocket with maddening deliberation and finally produced an envelope. 'It's this that brought me out, Chief Inspector — it was 'phoned through from Glasgow to the station at Kyle, and the constable who brought it over was told you were keen to get it.'

'I am.' Thane ripped the envelope open, took out the single-sheet message form it contained and read it through. When he'd finished, he glanced towards Moss.

'Phil — '

Moss read, grinned and thumbed towards Allowes, whose curiosity was growing by the moment. 'Will I — ?'

'Why not?' said Thane dryly. 'He's got a right to know.'

Frowning, Allowes grabbed the message form. He scanned the first few lines of writing, flushed angrily, and glared towards Thane.

'This — this is — '

'An outrage?' suggested Thane helpfully.

'Damn it, Thane — '

'I had to check,' said Thane bluntly. 'Even security men can go bent. Until I got that I'd only your story you were in London all weekend.'

'And now you know I was, at a ruddy Admiralty briefing conference.' Allowes refused to be mollified. 'What's this other business about how long I've been stationed in Clyde area?'

'Just three months and with the Australians at Woomera before that — you couldn't have been involved in the earlier leaks.' Thane pointed to the message form. 'Now read the rest, and stop steaming at the ears.'

Scowling, Allowes obeyed. The two Mill-side men saw his face change from anger to guarded, worried interest. He looked up.

'How much do you know about this, Thane?'

'Only that it's a list of firms who use Bart Kelly as their P.R. man . . . and that I want your reaction.'

'Kelly — ' the security man looked again at the paper in his hand and groaned. 'We know of positive security leaks from three of these places and we're worried about two more. That's spread over the last few years.' He balled his fists angrily. 'And Kelly — the privileged outsider, somebody any modern firm takes for granted yet — '

'Never screened?'

'I don't think so.' Allowes crossed over to the kitchen's shelves, seized the whisky bottle, and poured a stiff measure into a handy cup. He took a long swallow then sighed. 'I thought he saved your life, Thane.'

'He hadn't much choice — not if he wanted to keep his own and remain in circulation,' reminded Thane. 'He must have been using Hayston as his inside man. But Carter's death and having young Shaw hanging around would have Hayston trembling about his future.'

'So he got the girl to collect that stopwatch, giving him something of an alibi, then sneaked back and booby-trapped the place — ' Allowes nursed the cup in his hand, his manner dazed.

'We've got someone who saw a man heading from near the cottage towards the test slope,' Thane told him. 'Probably he meant Hayston to blow himself up when he came back in the evening, used the two charges to make sure, then had a lucky break when Hayston spilled that oil.'

'Eh — sir — ' Sergeant Kingsley, almost forgotten in the background, eased himself forward. 'Thon Hayston didn't spill the oil on himself. I thought you knew — it was Kelly who did it, then made a fuss about it bein' an accident. I wasn't far off when it happened.'

It was a small touch, but a final one. It left the big blank of Ian Shaw's meeting with Carter, the quirk of fate which had brought Carter's past home to roost at such a time. But the blanks could be filled, what mattered that now at least one of the patterns had shape, giving them cause and purpose for action.

'You made me a promise, Thane,' reminded Commander Allowes. 'You want a man for murder — two murders I suppose. But I think I've even more at stake.'

'Maybe.'

'You said you'd let him make the contact,' persisted Allowes.

'Who says he hasn't already?' demanded Moss.

'No.' The security man was strained but positive. 'I'll guarantee it.'

Thane shrugged. 'It won't harm things to wait a little — it could help us, come to that.' He roughed his thoughts aloud. 'I've got to see MacMaster, then I want Shaw. Suppose Phil and I use Sergeant Kingsley's car to go over to Broadford Hospital, then head back here. We'll leave Sergeant Kingsley with you to keep an eye on things at this end — and particularly on Kelly and Shaw when the Hydrostat bunch return to the hotel.' He grinned. 'Then maybe we can lean on Kelly a little, make him more anxious to contact your pal Koltsov.'

Allowes nodded his head in vigorous approval. 'Fine — excellent. Sergeant, you're agreeable?'

Sergeant Kingsley's eyes strayed towards the bottle. 'Och, it sounds very reasonable,' he agreed mildly. 'It'll just be a question of passing the time.'

8

There was only one way to Broadford Hospital, the inevitable, time-consuming drive along the shore-hugging route to Kyle of Lochalsh, across the water on the slow, blunt-nosed vehicle ferry to Skye, then more mileage along the island's narrow, almost empty main road. Colin Thane drove steadily while the rest flickered by — the old, thatched crofting cottages, the purple heather and yellow broom, the shaggy cattle which strayed on the edge of the tarmac.

But it meant the two Millside men had a chance to talk . . . and at last Phil Moss got round to the Splits Clark episode. His eyes still on the road, Thane chortled with delight.

'He's due up in court for remand today,' said Moss ruefully. 'In fact, he'll have been through by now. Emma Robertson's back home, of course — no charges, but she'll be on the witness list when he goes to trial.'

'How does she feel about it?' Thane horn-blasted again as they swung round a bend and scattered a handful of young Highland steers.

Moss sighed. 'I 'phoned this morning, from

the airport. She still doesn't know I started the ball rolling — but according to her it's all a big mistake and Splits is an innocent victim.'

The rest had been a short, sharp monologue on the way she'd been treated, ending with the fact that she had to go back to Headquarters for a further interview — 'and this time I'll have my lawyer with me, Philip.'

A vision of what that might mean kept him in a gloomy silence for the rest of the journey.

Broadford Hospital sat snug at the head of a sheltered bay, looking out towards the grey-blue sea and with a background of green hills rising fast to meet the massive, sullen peaks of the Cuillin mountains. They parked the car, went in, and enlisted a young, crisply starched nurse as guide.

Professor MacMaster was in the medical residents' lounge. A gaunt, bony figure with a face which seemed to crack each time his lips moved, he sat in an armchair near the window sipping tea from the matron's best china with the complete air of one who was undisputed monarch of all he surveyed.

'I expected you earlier,' he said pointedly, balancing cup and saucer in his long, thin fingers. 'Still, I've finished my own task — the Hayston post mortem. Very simple, straightforward case of death, no comments of importance. You'll get my report.'

'I'm glad you could come,' said Thane warily.

MacMaster sucked his teeth and gave the equivalent of a smile. 'A pleasant little out-of-town jaunt is always welcome, you know. A break from routine refreshes, invigorates the mind. Don't you agree, Moss?'

Phil Moss mumbled politely.

'What you told Phil Moss interested me, interested me more than a little,' declared Thane, anxious to keep down the preliminaries.

'Did it?' The elderly forensic expert took another sip of his tea, which was weak and milky. 'However, I imagine it would have been less unexpected if you'd studied my earlier report with proper care.'

'Perhaps.' Thane restrained himself. The MacMaster legend had been built up on over a generation of such confrontations, and he'd no intention of providing the material for a new addition to the forensic expert's acid stock of after-dinner stories.

'Sit down,' invited MacMaster. 'Some tea?'

They shook their heads, pulled chairs across, and settled beside him.

'Now, the position in lay terminology.'

MacMaster tooth-sucked again. 'My report with the — ah — assistance of Doctor Williams said the time of death in the case of William Carter could be only a rough approximation. I believe, however, that your detective work does suggest the subject left home about noon. If we co-relate that to the stomach contents and other medical data available death probably occurred some time between late afternoon and late evening. Correct?'

'Until now,' growled Thane, wishing he'd get to the point.

'Exactly.' His eyes darted from one man to the other in quick, bird-like style. 'I think we can alter that a little. On our flight up, Moss indicated that the bloodstains found at the Hydrostat factory constituted a puzzle — I'm paraphrasing his words. My view is that it would be wrong to presume the bloodstains necessarily occurred in what one might term the commissioning of Carter's death, even though some of them were on his clothing.'

Thane frowned. 'You mean there could have been a punch-up at the plant earlier?'

'Earlier, but on the same day,' agreed MacMaster. 'There was a slight graze on Carter's forehead and a small cut on his inner lip — both mentioned in my report, both possibly caused in a fist fight. I instructed my technicians to prepare tissue sections from the two areas. That takes time, gentlemen, a full twenty-four to thirty-six-hour period before the final slides are ready.'

It was a laborious preparation, one Thane had watched more than once. Time, skill and patience went into the process of cleansing the specimens, embedding them in wax, bringing them on to the final delicate work of the microtome which shaved wafer-thin sections of a mere thousandth of a millimetre.

'The slides were available late yesterday and I myself, naturally, carried out the microscopic examination.' MacMaster selected his words, as if lecturing a brace of rather backward but not completely hopeless students. 'It is an established textbook fact that the healing of wounds in the living human body follows a fixed pattern. One expects an initial degree of cellular infiltration from six hours onwards, this to be well apparent at between twelve and eighteen hours. Later one observes new capillaries beginning to form at approximately thirty-six hours and so on — the full calendar is sufficient to constitute a forensic thesis.'

'This healing, Professor' — Phil Moss struggled with the concept tossed in their laps — 'does it come to a stop when a man dies?'

'Not like this.' MacMaster brought his cup

sharply against its saucer. 'More like this.' He repeated the action but in a slower, gentle fashion. 'Body cell activity lingers for a little, but is soon extinguished. Our pattern isn't affected.

'In Carter's case there was sufficient cellular infiltration in the slide specimens to make it clear both minor wounds were caused from six to eight hours before death. I'm inclined to favour the lesser figure, but it is minimum.' He sat back, as if waiting for applause.

'It fits.' Thane took a deep breath. 'You've no idea just how well it fits, Professor. I know one young man who owes you a vote of thanks — you've taken him off the hook.'

'I trust you've — ah — someone else waiting for the vacancy?' queried MacMaster dryly.

Thane nodded grimly.

★ ★ ★

Their return journey to the Kyle ferry was through a fresh drizzle, with the car's wipers sweeping in hypnotic fashion. They reached the slipway in time to be the last vehicle squeezed aboard a ferry ready to leave, and shared the short trip with a milk tanker and an assortment of smaller transport. On the far side, as the Austin's wheels touched mainland again, Phil Moss leaned forward in the passenger seat, peering through the rain-streaked windscreen.

'Colin — '

'I know.' Thane had already seen the scarlet Mercedes parked just beyond the ferry area. He steered the Austin towards it and stopped in front. Commander Allowes left the car and came towards them, while Sergeant Kingsley, snug under the coupe's hood, waved a wry greeting through the glass.

'We've got trouble,' said Allowes without ceremony, opening one of the rear doors and swinging himself into the seat behind them. 'I'm damned glad to see you.'

'Koltsov?' queried Thane quietly.

'Not yet — it's Bart Kelly.'

Moss swore softly and demanded, 'What's happened?'

'I'm not sure yet.' Allowes' moon-like face radiated an equal mixture of anxiety and indecision. 'We went to the Glenpeak hotel, to check when Stanley's crew were expected back. The reception clerk told us we'd just missed Kelly — he'd arrived out of the blue, collected his luggage, and checked out.'

Thane grunted, with little need to imagine how the little security man has reacted to that item of news. 'Checked with David Stanley yet?'

'Of course.' Allowes was pained at the possible inference. 'We went straight out, met his people on their way back from the Pass of Cattle site. According to him, they'd just finished at the test slope and were ready to move their gear on to the Pass when Kelly announced he wouldn't be coming. He said he was still feeling pretty rough after the bombing business, and was going back to Glasgow.'

'What's he driving?' asked Moss.

'That old station wagon. Sergeant Kingsley's put out an alert, and the county cars are watching the main roads south. They've orders to report if he's sighted but not to stop him.'

Thane sat silent for a long moment, watching the thin, drizzling rain blanket the world outside the car's glass and metal shell. Then he asked, 'What about Shaw?'

'Does he matter now?' scowled Allowes. 'He's at the new test base, doing his night watchman act with another of the Hydrostat people. Look, Kelly's the man we want — '

'And we can both guess where he's heading,' said Thane calmly. 'Where's your pal Koltsov staying tonight?'

'The same place as before, the Sunbiggin

Hotel — it's north of here, on the other side of Loch Carron.' Allowes fidgeted in his seat. 'I'd like to get out there.'

'North of here — ' Colin Thane took the area map Kingsley carried in the car's glove box, studied it for a moment, then nodded. 'It takes us nearer to Shaw. You lead the way, and we'll follow.'

The Mercedes in the lead, the Austin close on its tail, they covered the twelve-mile distance at a pace which Thane found close to alarming. It was, like all the rest, a wild road and a lonely road, part desolate moorland, part rock-fringed coast where here and there a brightly coloured tent had been pitched by some hardy camper. At Strome, where the sea-loch shrank to a narrow neck of water, there was another ferry crossing, slow and cumbersome.

The Sunbiggin Hotel was about four miles on — a tall, castle-styled structure reached by a length of private road and set close by the loch's shore. They stopped the cars before the last bend of the driveway and Commander Allowes walked on alone.

He was back within a few minutes, a worried man.

'Well?' demanded Thane.

'I don't like it.' Allowes took the cigarette Thane offered, accepted a light, and took a

264

long, reflective draw. 'Kelly certainly hasn't shown up. But there was a minor panic just over an hour back, and my people are just beginning to wonder if they've been played for fools.'

He told it grimly, his shoulders hunched, his face bleak. Alexis Koltsov had announced that he felt tired and would be staying in his hotel suite for the rest of the day. The Scottish Office guide passed the word to the two men Allowes had placed on watch and they'd stayed on their toes.

'Next thing they knew, that damned black Zis bashed away from the hotel with three men aboard. They left the Scottish Office bod here and went after it in their own car.' Allowes grimaced. 'The Zis toured every apology for a track in the district for almost half an hour without stopping, then came back.'

'But no Koltsov aboard?' murmured Thane.

'No Koltsov. Out pops the chauffeur and a couple of locals he'd taken for a drive. And when the Scottish Office man asks to see Koltsov in his suite that damned secretary-interpreter answers the door and politely tells him he can't that his boss is resting. He swears he heard Koltsov's voice from somewhere inside, but — '

'Isn't that enough, sir?' asked Kingsley. 'I mean, if the man's there — '

'Is he?' Allowes gave a black scowl. 'Ever used a tape recorder, Sergeant? It's an old, simple trick — part two of how to be a spy in six easy lessons.'

'And a diploma if you don't get caught,' grunted Moss in acid fashion. 'Well, can't we go in and find out?'

'Not unless you'd really like to start a first-class diplomatic row,' snapped Allowes. 'Listen, Moss, you and Thane are thief-takers and it may seem plain and simple what we should do. But this is different — '

'Is it?' asked Thane. His rugged face split in a sudden, cheerful grin. 'Like you said, Moss and I are thief-takers. And a thief can pop up anywhere.'

'Eh?' The security man saw the wink which passed between the two detectives and felt suddenly uneasy. 'Now wait — '

'You wait. Get back in your car, sit down, and finish that cigarette,' advised Thane blithely. 'Where's Koltsov's suite?'

'Top floor right, suite B, but — '

'We won't be long.' Thane glanced towards Kingsley and advised the county man. 'You'd better stay out of this, Sergeant.'

'In my own area, sir?' Kingsley was indignant at the thought. 'Like hell I will.'

They left Allowes where he was, walked down the driveway, entered the hotel, and stopped for a moment to get their bearings in the foyer. The reception clerk left his desk and came towards them.

'Police,' said Thane shortly.

'Well — ' the clerk frowned. 'If it's Commander Allowes you want — '

'Never heard of him,' declared Thane. 'This won't take long.' While the clerk still gaped, the three men marched up the stairway to the top floor and stopped outside the door to suite B.

'Ready?' murmured Thane. He lifted his fist and rapped sharply on the door. When it opened, the burly secretary-interpreter looked out.

'I am sorry,' he began in carefully accented English. 'I have orders — '

'Police.' Thane flashed his warrant card fractionally under the man's nose, shouldered him aside, and strode into the room beyond. It was furnished as a lounge, and Koltsov's chauffeur, his tunic unbuttoned, sprang up from an armchair.

'We have diplomatic privilege — ' the secretary threw himself forward as the three men headed for the first of the bedroom doors.

'Sorry, sir — ' Phil Moss collided with him

in clumsy fashion. The man staggered back, tripped over Sergeant Kingsley's foot, and went sprawling.

The chauffeur was made of sterner stuff. He growled as he moved in front of the doorway, his body halfway to a fighting crouch.

'Nobody sees — '

'We do.' Thane stepped deliberately forward, blocked the chopping right-hand blow which came his way, and grinned as the man tried to butt him. Millside Division was a hard training school, where one cop was regarded as sufficient to take care of a mob of bloody-minded neds any Saturday night. He let the man come on again, side-stepped, and hit him once where neck met shoulder. The chauffeur lurched and fell into Kingsley's waiting arms.

The bedroom on the other side of the door was empty. So were the other two rooms in the suite. But there was a small battery-powered tape recorder lying in one. Moss switched it on, and Thane smiled without humour as Koltsov's voice chattered gaily from the moving spool.

'Enough, Phil.' He waited until Moss clicked the switch, then led the way back to the outer room, where the two Embassy men sat scowling side by side on a couch with

Sergeant Kingsley standing alongside.

'Whoever you are, this will be reported!' Koltsov's secretary spat the words, rising to his feet.

'Sorry again,' said Thane, mildly repentant. 'But I told you who we were. We'd a report that a wanted man had been seen in the hotel — '

'A violent wanted man,' agreed Moss, spoiling the effect by grinning like a monkey. 'Looks like we were wrong, though.'

'And of course, we wouldn't dream of disturbing guests if it wasn't for their own safety,' declared Thane. 'Correct, Sergeant?'

'Aye, we've got to ensure safety, sir,' said Kingsley heavily. He appealed to the two men at his side. 'Is that not how it should be?'

The chauffeur spat an answer. Thane didn't know the language, but the meaning was clear.

'And the same to you,' he agreed cheerfully.

* * *

Allowes was fretting by the roadside when they returned to the cars. He read all he wanted to know in Thane's face and sighed. 'Damn him. All right, what now?'

'That's worrying me a little,' confessed Thane.

'A little?' Allowes purpled. 'We've lost Kelly, we've lost Koltsov — '

'Two down and one to go,' said Thane quietly, but with a cold edge to the words. 'I'm thinking of Ian Shaw.'

'But he's more or less cleared — '

'We know it, but they don't.' He waited till the security man had simmered down a little. 'That's our only advantage. They're still likely to be gambling we'll concentrate on young Shaw as our candidate.'

'Even if they are, what difference does it make?' Allowes was restlessly impatient.

'Take it that Koltsov's got nerve enough to want the final evaluation figures on the hydrostatic transmission tests — his last collection as the postman. Then he decides that the way things are going he can't wait for them. He's being watched, Kelly's position is dangerous — well, I know the choice I'd see in his shoes. Either cut my losses and get out, or go for the jackpot.'

'What jackpot?' Allowes froze at the words.

'I'd pinch either the truck or the car,' said Thane calmly. 'That's what any self-respecting ned would do.'

'You can't be — damn it, I believe you really are serious!' Allowes took time to recover from the enormity of the idea. Then, sardonically, he demanded, 'And what would your tame thug do with this stolen vehicle, Thane? Have a freight plane sit down on some mountain-top and collect it — or have a nice, handy giant submarine pop up at the Kyle slipway? Talk sense, man!'

'He doesn't have to keep it for long,' snapped Thane. 'All he needs is to get it, then dismantle one of the drive cylinder valve units. They're what matter, the only things that make the system different from half a dozen other brands.'

'But could he do it, sir — on his own, like?' asked Sergeant Kingsley, respectfully sceptical.

'Maybe the Commander's the best one to answer that,' murmured Phil Moss. 'Remember, we're just three thief-taking cops.'

'Well, Commander?' Thane waited, his face impassive.

The security man swallowed hard and gave a slow nod. 'It's — possible,' he agreed reluctantly. Then his head jerked up. 'Well, why stand here? Let's find out.'

*   *   *

They drove north again, north into country wilder than any they'd yet travelled. The grey

271

cloud was breaking a little, giving patches of clear sky and an occasional glimpse of approaching sunset. The road, flat and narrow, wound like an untidy ribbon through a low funnel of a valley with the dark mountains squatting close on either side. This was Nature Conservancy territory, where man held a slender toehold and left the rest to the wildcat and deer, the occasional majestic eagle and the black-winged carrion crow. Dull and desolate, almost prehistoric in its brooding, the land seemed to sneer at their road and brood at their passing.

With Kingsley as his guide, Allowes led the way. Indicator winking, the red Mercedes swung left on to a lesser route and almost immediately began climbing. A few yards behind, Colin Thane took a deep breath and dropped down a gear as the road ahead ate steadily upwards. This was the route most people only heard about, the Pass of Cattle, the Bealach-Na-Ba in an older tongue, five and a half miles of dizzy, upwards multiple bends, of hairpin brinks, of occasional safety fences and edging dykes, of ominous gaps and awesome downward visions.

'Hell, it's weirdsome,' admitted Moss, glancing out of his passenger window then quickly switching his attention inboard. 'Remember the story of the bloke with the furniture truck — '

'Shut up.'

He remembered all right. The truck driver had come north with his load, somehow struggled his giant vehicle over the Bealach-Na-Ba to its destination, the isolated village of Applecross, then had flatly refused to make the return journey with his empty vehicle. His firm finally got their vehicle back by sending a replacement driver north, bringing their first man out as a reluctant passenger.

Maybe it wasn't all that bad. He changed down to second gear, watched the car ahead screw-thread its way round a tighter hairpin, then cursed and braked as he realised his own mistaken line. It took an inching forward-reverse-forward manoeuvre to wriggle round, then the Austin's engine had to work hard in bottom gear to catch up once more. They were high enough now for the broken cloud to wisp around them, the rays of the setting sun stabbing past like living silk to disappear far below. Out of the corner of his eye he saw Moss fumble in a pocket, a hand go to his lips, then heard a steady, earnest crunching coming from his second-in-command's mouth.

But at last the Mercedes' indicators winked again and he followed as it swung off on a rough track leading into a tiny glen formed by two flanking shoulders of the mountain range. They found the Hydrostat camp about a quarter of a mile in, a rough semi-circle of vehicles drawn close to the shelter of the rocks. As they drew nearer, Thane counted them off — a transporter and trailers, two mobile workshops, and the grey Hydrostat saloon.

'But no truck,' said Moss, his voice empty of all emotion.

They drew in behind the other car as it stopped then got out and joined Allowes and Kingsley. Nothing stirred and the only sound in the little glen was the rush of water on some tumbling mountain burn and the gentle sigh of the wind.

Allowes rubbed his jaw and sighed wearily. 'Late again — well, let's get it over with. That green trailer is the one fitted out for their night guards.'

The four-wheeled trailer had a flight of steps leading up to its doorway and a faint wisp of smoke still rising from the short stack of its solid-fuel stove. Sergeant Kingsley, the first man to reach the door, found it locked. He took a half-step back, slammed his weight against it, and almost tumbled through as it gave.

They went inside, peering around the shadowed interior until Moss found the switch to the battery-powered lights.

Danny Benson lay sprawled untidily, face down, on the lower of the two bunks situated across the width of the trailer's tail. Thane bent over him, his mouth a tight line at the sight of the congealed blood matted thick on the elderly mechanic's head. Benson's wrists were tied behind his back and as Thane bent lower he heard the man's faint, shallow breathing.

Allowes had a knife, a big, old-fashioned seaman's clasp with a black bone handle. The sharp steel sliced through the cords and they carefully eased the man round on his back.

'He's had a damned hard thump,' breathed Sergeant Kingsley. He moved back and reappeared with some water in an old, blackened kettle. Thane soaked his handkerchief in the water, squeezed a few drops against Benson's mouth, then laid the cold cloth against his forehead.

Benson moaned and stirred a little, then his eyelids fluttered.

'What happened, Danny?' asked Thane, his lips close to the man's ear. But Benson only groaned again then slid back into unconsciousness.

Thane sighed and rose. 'No sense in trying him. Kingsley, you'd better get on that radio.'

'Not from here, sir,' said the county man

275

ruefully. 'The mountains blot out any kind of signal. It means getting to a telephone.'

'Then we're on our own for the moment.' Thane scowled, his mind racing. 'My bet is they've taken Shaw along with them, to give us a nice, handy suspect. But they wouldn't have a long enough lead to get back down the Pass without meeting us. Where else could they go?'

Kingsley had no need to ponder. 'There's a pretty limited choice, sir. The mountain road goes on to Applecross village and stops. They would have to take a boat or use the shore tracks to go further — though the tracks are out for anything bigger than a motorbike. The only other thing they could try is to use the Falls Way. It's an old road that goes off to the right about half a mile further up the pass. It's in a pretty poor state, but — '

'Where does it lead?'

'Well, if — if, mark you — you took it, you'd come back down to the east of here, clear of the mountains, and could cut across to the main road south.' Kingsley shrugged. 'I've never been along it myself, but I know it gets its name from some o' the waterfalls you see along the way.'

Commander Allowes gnawed his lip. 'Koltsov could be trying to get back to the hotel. He's got nerve enough to play it that way, then sit back and laugh.'

'The Applecross road would be the only route for that,' pronounced Kingsley. 'He'd have to dump the truck when he got there, but wi' any sort of boat or a bike — '

Thane made up his mind. 'You and Kingsley take it, Commander. And the first 'phone you get to, organise an ambulance for here and try to get something resembling road blocks set up. Moss and I will try this Falls road.'

'What about Benson?' queried Allowes, glancing at the man in the bunk. 'Can we leave him — just like that?'

Thane nodded. Until skilled help arrived, Danny Benson was in as safe a place as any — and any premature attempt to move him held its own dangers.

★   ★   ★

A minute later they set off. Half a mile on, where the route forked, the two cars parted company and Thane found himself driving over a rough and broken surface which led along the side of a dark overhang of rock. Phil Moss winced in the passenger seat as the car bounced over the potholes, and felt no better when, beyond the overhang, they began to climb again.

Looking ahead, he could see the last red glow of sunset glinting on long threads of water hurrying down the mountain slopes — and their route's hairpin path, bends coiling one above the other. He heard Thane curse as the car's tyres scrubbed inches from the edge of a savage drop, and knew the Millside chief's hands were knuckle-tight on that steering wheel.

Suddenly, for the first time, Thane gave a thin whistle and nodded ahead. At the track's edge a little way ahead tyre tracks had left their mark on the soft shoulder of the road before vanishing into harder, level ground beyond, a level shoulder which disappeared from sight round yet another rocky outcrop. He stopped the car alongside and glanced at Moss.

'Two sets, Phil — but different, the truck and Kelly's station wagon. Ready?'

'If it gets me out of this thing, yes.' Moss was ready to welcome the devil himself as a reasonable alternative to the Falls Way.

They left the car and began walking, finding fresh traces of the tyre tracks as they went along the shoulder, picking their way carefully in the failing light. Then, so simply that it would have been comical in another time and place, Moss slipped. The patch of rock was smooth-grained and silver-grey, the green lichen which ate across it was deceptively springy, and where the wiry Millside man had been moving confidently one moment, he'd crashed down the next. He tried to rise to his feet then sank down again with a suppressed yelp of pain.

'Let's see it.' Thane squatted down beside him, eased off his companion's left shoe, and sighed. Moss's ankle was already beginning to swell in the classic style of a major sprain. He glanced at the offending shoe and his sympathy evaporated as he saw the thin sole and worn-down heel. 'You're lucky you didn't break your ruddy neck. Can you make it back to the car?'

'In my own time.' Moss dragged himself into a more comfortable position, gritting his teeth in the process. 'Going on?'

'What else?'

'Watch it then — the pension fund's pretty low.' As a joke it was weak, but Thane knew what he meant. He gave a slight grin, rose, and walked on.

Beyond the outcrop's bulk Thane moved with a new deliberate caution. The tyre tracks were still there, marking a perilous way along a rough but level area of small broken rock debris, an area little more than an accidental wrinkle in the mountainside with here and there an occasional stunted clump of gorsebush. He had no illusions about what might wait ahead. Koltsov and his companion were professionals in a business where winner took all — and where the loser seldom had a second chance.

The wrinkle twisted into a slight rise. He crawled to the top then sank down on his stomach and drew a deep breath. Down below, less than a hundred yards ahead, the canvas roofed Hydrostat truck and Kelly's station wagon were stopped side by side in a saucer-like hollow. A figure worked beside the truck, and he heard the faint clink of metal on metal. One man — where there should be two. He stayed where he was, puzzled, tensely alert, straining his eyes against the gathering dusk. The vague shape of the mountain misted a little, and he felt a sudden splash of rain against his face.

Slowly, every nerve signalling him to give up and get out, he began wriggling forward over the broken surface while the rain began to patter down and the figure by the truck worked on. Twenty yards from the vehicles the signals had become alarm calls. But he was committed. Thane gathered himself for a rush forward, then froze as a foot crunched on the loose rocks behind him.

'Let's get up nice and easily,' invited Kelly's

voice. 'In fact, let's not do anything in a hurry.'

It had happened. He felt the tension give way to an icy, fatalistic calm as he rose and turned.

Bart Kelly stood a short distance away, close to the clump of gorse where he'd been waiting. The nine millimetre Mauser automatic in his hand pointed steadily and his face held a cynical grin. Down by the truck the other man had stopped play-acting.

'Walk,' invited Kelly. 'And remember, there's little profit in being a dead hero.'

'Your old mother said that?' asked Thane with a sigh.

'No, but this does.' Kelly moved the Mauser a fraction.

'Was her name really Kelly?'

'Does it matter?' The man thumbed. 'Let's go.'

As they reached the truck Alexis Koltsov met them with a frown. 'There's only the one?'

'He's all I've seen,' said Kelly briefly. 'This is Thane.' He stepped closer, used his free hand to search the Millside man's clothing, extracted Thane's short wooden baton and handcuffs, then nodded. 'That's the lot.'

'Just the little stick? It seems so — so primitive.' Koltsov shook his head. 'I'm sorry you have come, Mr Thane.'

'You left the hotel before we could ask for a formal invite, Mr Koltsov,' said Thane mildly.

'So that is how things are.' Koltsov's face stayed calm. 'Well, it was a clumsy ruse — perhaps this was inevitable.' He glanced at Kelly. 'These handcuffs look efficient.'

Kelly grinned a little, gestured Thane to put his hands behind his back, and snapped the metal cuffs round the detective's wrists. As an afterthought he made another search of Thane's pockets, found the handcuff key, and tossed it away.

'Go back towards the road — make sure he was alone,' ordered Koltsov. As Kelly trotted off, he inspected Thane once more. 'I have a gun, too, Chief Inspector. So please, no trouble — and let me show you why we were ready.'

Pushed by the shoulder, Thane let himself be led to the far edge of the little plateau and saw for himself. Through the misting rain the mountain's slope, harsh and rockstrewn, fell far and dizzily below. Halfway down he could plainly see the ribbon of the Falls Way road.

'From there to where we turned off up here is a good seven or eight minutes travel,' mused Koltsov. One hand gathered the collar of his jacket close against the rain, the other gripped a significant bulge in his pocket.

'Back to the truck now. You have company there.'

He herded Thane back to the vehicle. The tailboard was down and inside, his back against the cab's shell, Ian Shaw lay tied hand and foot. He met Thane's gaze with a rueful grimace.

'Inside, please.' Koltsov waited while Thane made an awkward job of climbing aboard. 'And back — ' he nodded as he was obeyed, swung aboard in one smooth easy action, then wiped the rain from his sallow face and gave a sigh. 'Here, at least, you will be dry.'

'You want us to thank you?' demanded Shaw bitterly, no hope in his eyes.

'Things could be worse, my friend.' Koltsov glanced from the young engineer to Thane, his bright eyes thoughtful. 'For you, at any rate, they could be much worse. Chief Inspector, you will lie down, please.' As Thane hesitated, he brought his hand from his pocket and with it a Mauser the twin of Kelly's weapon. 'Now.'

Thane obeyed. The slim Cultural Attaché lifted a length of cord from one corner of the truck and made a rough but adequate one-handed job of tying his ankles. He stood back, inspected his handiwork and grimaced. 'It will do. Now, until Kelly returns to confirm you came alone I have work to do.'

He moved back to the tailboard, dropped down into the rain and vanished from sight.

'And that's that,' said Thane ruefully. 'How are you, lad?'

'All right.' Shaw gnawed his lip. 'How — how's Danny Benson?'

'He should live.' Thane eased himself into a more comfortable position, tried the hand-cuffs, and knew there was no easy escape from their grip. They were tightly secure. 'What happened down there?'

The young engineer flushed at the memory. 'Danny and I were in the trailer when these two burst in. One of them stuck a gun in my ribs, the other belted Danny over the head like he was taking a spoon to an egg and — well, as far as I can make out they brought me along to be the original decoy duck.'

'Blame yourself for it,' grunted Thane. 'Jane Maulden told us most of the story, which is one of the reasons we got this far — '

'We?' Shaw seized on the word.

'Me on my own as far as this place is concerned,' corrected Thane steadily. 'I was playing a longshot — and it backfired.' His mind was on Phil Moss, crawling back to their car, with a vision superimposed of Kelly loping along in the same direction, gun in hand. 'Why the devil didn't you tell us you'd been at the Hydrostat plant on Sunday and had a tussle with Carter?'

'How would it sound till now?' protested Shaw. He squirmed round to meet Thane's gaze. 'If Jane's told you the rest you'll know I met him there by arrangement. First he wanted more time to think what he could do to square things with Jane's father. I said a share in the company or cash on the nail, he started telling me I'd no real proof. Then he tried to thump me with a wrench.' He shrugged. 'I thumped him instead and — and — '

'Took his keys and shoved him into the enamelling oven,' completed Thane grimly.

'Something like that, but I only did it to keep him out of my hair,' protested Shaw. 'Then I had a prowl around his office, and went through his desk. Carter was all set to sell out his share of the firm. I saw the letters — he was ditching Stanley, his wife, the lot. He'd a passport and air tickets ready, all the way to Mexico.'

'And all because of you,' nodded Thane. 'How much of this squeeze was going to end up in your pocket?'

'Nothing,' snapped Shaw fiercely. 'I reckoned old Maulden needed it more than I did. I've seen the poor old devil. Maybe at first I thought I'd end up with a slice of the take, but not after that.' He scowled at the idea. 'Another thing, I left Carter in the oven but I didn't throw the switch — that's the truth.'

'It is indeed!' Alexis Koltsov peered in at them from the tailboard then scrambled up into shelter. 'I was — ah — eavesdropping, Chief Inspector,' he said almost apologetically. 'I wondered if you really did come alone. But that is settled, eh? Kelly is on his way back, and for the rest — ' he shook his head. 'I think you know already who disposed of Carter. Kelly is a good man for us, but you showed no surprise at finding him here.'

He turned as footsteps sounded above the patter of rain and a moment later gave Bart Kelly a helping hand aboard. The man was wet and shivering, yet seemed satisfied.

'The car's there, but I didn't see anyone,' he reported.

'Good.' Koltsov nodded briefly. 'I heard Mr Thane confirm it to our young friend — and I have just been confirming his belief that you were the one who disposed of Carter.'

Kelly's mouth fell open. Then he recovered, gave a knowing look, and hefted his gun significantly. 'Well, maybe it doesn't matter now, eh?' He glanced towards Thane and spoke almost sadly. 'Nothing personal, Chief Inspector — in fact, I was becoming almost fond of you and your pal Moss.'

'But why did you have to kill Carter?' persisted Thane, a fresh relief in his mind at the man's empty-handed return.

It was Koltsov who replied. 'Bart — ah — visited the plant on the Sunday, late on. He was making what would probably have been a last call — his future was uncertain.'

'That's a twisted way of saying Carter was pretty well on to me,' grunted Kelly, shaking more of the rain from his clothes. 'He'd been quizzing Peter Hayston about me — and Hayston was in a panic because of a little arrangement we'd had about keys and the current safe combination. My guess is that's why Carter was calling his wife and Stanley back home — to decide what to do about it all, and maybe use it as another lever to force them to sell out. I knew about that side of things, too — Hayston's ear was pretty close to the ground.' He gave a twisted grin. 'So when I heard someone banging on a door and saw Carter in that enamelling oven it was made to order.'

'And Hayston?'

'He worried too much.' Kelly seemed to regard it as sufficient explanation.

Koltsov stirred, growing impatient. 'We have a job to finish, Bart. As soon as that valve unit is removed it will be time to go — before we have more visitors.'

'And them?'

'I'm not sure.' Koltsov looked at his prisoners strangely, then beckoned to Kelly. 'We'll talk about it.'

They left the truck. Seconds later, the clink of metal on metal began from somewhere beneath the vehicle's chassis.

'They'll talk about us,' mimicked Shaw cynically. 'I can guess what that means.'

'We're in one piece so far,' mused Thane more hopefully than he felt. 'And if it works out — well, you're in the clear now.'

'Thanks.' Shaw found it slender comfort.

'Did you know Hayston was working for them?'

Shaw shook his head. 'No. I got the story about how Carter pirated old Maulden's work once I'd put a little pressure on him — but not the rest. After the Sunday, Hayston thought the best way to keep himself out of trouble was to keep me in the clear. That's why he fixed the job for me — and he let me know he'd Carter's desk diary handy if I ever got too tough.' He stared down at the truck's floor, as if he could see the men beneath. 'Still, I managed to talk him into photo-copying some of the company records the night they were out of the cashier's safe.'

'Why?'

'Just an idea a page or two of the early stuff

288

might help show Carter had been on the crook. I'd still a hope I might get round to telling David Stanley about old Maulden's work — Stanley's straight enough.' Shaw found a faint humour in what had happened. 'Then, of course, Hayston dam' nearly got caught — but when he showed me that picture of you it seemed a lovely chance to pay you back for that grilling I'd had.'

'I — ' Thane stopped and frowned. The sounds beneath them had stopped. Shaw looked at him, swallowed hard, and stayed silent. Above the constant patter of the rain they heard the estate car's door open and close then Koltsov appeared at the truck's tailgate, the same strange expression on his face.

'We're going,' he said in a quiet voice. 'I have had — well, a discussion with Kelly. Originally we planned for Shaw to disappear, Chief Inspector, and for you to spend a very long time seeking him. It isn't hard to hide a body in this desolation. But' — he smiled a little — 'with so much known that is finished. I do not believe in unnecessary killing. We will move your car in off the road, but you should be found before too many hours have passed.'

'And you?' asked Thane, his mouth still dry.

Koltsov gave a weary shrug. 'I have my delivery, my last I'm afraid, to make at a certain place. It is arranged. Kelly will go with it — his career is finished and the offer makes him more willing to do what I say.' He gave the same thin smile, raised one hand in a faint salute, and turned away.

They lay listening, still uncertain, until the estate car's engine started and they heard the vehicle growl away, tyres crunching over the broken rock. Ian Shaw's relief came in a long, shuddering sigh.

'I feel pretty much the same,' mused Thane. 'Now shut up for a minute.'

'But — '

'Quiet.' He strained his ears then grinned. Someone was outside, moving towards them at a slow, dragging pace.

'But you said — ' Shaw stared at him accusingly.

'Of course I did.' Then pursed his lips and gave a quick whistle. It was echoed from outside and a moment later, wincing at the effort, Phil Moss drew himself painfully over the tailboard.

'What kept you?' queried Thane happily.

'I'm not used to hopping, and I scare easily when I see characters heading my way with guns.' Moss chuckled as he saw the handcuffs, produced his key, and released the bracelets. He left Thane to remove the rope from his legs while he used a penknife to cut Shaw loose. 'Well, do we go after them?'

'In the truck?' Thane shook his head. 'They'll have fixed it — and our car.'

'I thought they were going to fix you for a spell,' grunted Moss, a rare trace of emotion in his voice.

Thane nodded, rubbing his wrists. Koltsov had talked of a delivery arranged, yet originally he'd also hoped to get back to his hotel. That had to mean a delivery to the coast, which in turn meant going back down the Falls Way.

He gave a sudden snap of his fingers and jumped to his feet. 'Phil, you've done your part. Now if Shaw and I could push this thing to the edge and over — '

'Hell, yes!' Ian Shaw's eyes glinted at the prospect. 'It would keep on going till it hit the road. Is there time?'

'If we're lucky — and it would take a devil of a lot of loose rock with it. Check the handbrake's off and we'll start shoving.'

While Shaw raced round to the truck's cab Thane helped his second-in-command limp his way clear. Then, ignoring the rain, he hurried over to the edge of the little plateau and peered down through the semi-darkness. The station wagon's sidelights gleamed far below, heading along the road at a steady pace, but with still some distance to go.

'Thane — we're in luck!' Ian Shaw scrambled to join him, a savage grin on his face. 'They smashed the distributor, but there's no need to push. I can wind her over on the starter motor!'

'Then do it — but remember to jump.'

Shaw nodded, ran back, and jumped into the cab. There was a harsh whirr as the starter pinion engaged then in a slow, hiccuping, protesting fashion the truck began moving a ponderous few inches at a time towards the edge. It hiccuped again, the front wheels went over the edge then, as the whole vehicle began to slide, Shaw threw himself clear.

The truck slid on, gaining speed, bouncing crazily on its wheels for a distance before it hit a rock twice the size of a man, somersaulted, and began rolling. A growing mass of debris thundered down in its path, gaining momentum every second that passed in its long, deep fall.

Far down there, like some child's toy, the station wagon still travelled on. Thane gauged its speed and forced himself to keep watching. Unless the two men soon saw their danger . . .

Suddenly, they did. The station wagon

braked and skidded, then its lights disappeared as the avalanche of shattered truck, rock and mountain debris burst across the road in an awesome, foaming wave then poured on, its noise fading to a distant rumble as it carried on towards the valley below.

One hand clutching tight on Thane's shoulder for support, Phil Moss sucked hard on his teeth at the sight. Beside them, Ian Shaw licked lips which were dry despite the steady downpour of rain. Each one of them was, in his own way, hypnotised by the sheer violence of what had happened. But the spell was broken as a first lick of yellow flame rose far below. It spread, blossoming like some giant, flaring matchhead, then hardened into a steadily burning beacon.

It took Colin Thane a full ten minutes to reach the roadway, where the skeleton of the shattered station wagon still glowed cherry-red, its burned-out bodywork half-buried in the great mass of rubble and rock.

He slowed as he approached it then stopped, feeling sick. He hadn't meant this to happen, yet even if he'd known it would . . .

'Over here, Chief Inspector,' said a voice weakly.

Alexis Koltsov, half-sat, half-lay slumped against a great boulder which had come to a halt a few yards from the rest, close to the road's edge. The Cultural Attaché's clothes were torn and singed, the glow from the fire played strange tricks with the dark shadow of blood which ran from a deep cut on his forehead. His gun was in his left hand. He looked at Thane, forced a faint smile, and tossed the weapon far out over the slope. It clattered on a rock, and slid further down.

'I have, I think, a broken arm,' said Koltsov carefully. 'But that is all — for now, anyway. The price can be heavy for an error of judgement, Chief Inspector. You were not alone after all.'

'No.' Thane pursed his lips. 'What about Kelly?'

Koltsov gave a long, deep sigh. 'He didn't get out. It is difficult when your legs are trapped — and it will be hard for me to forget.'

'I'm sorry.' Thane found his cigarettes, lit one, and put it in the man's mouth. The bright eyes thanked him enough.

'These things happen.' Koltsov moved and winced a little. 'In the circumstances, it was perhaps just as well. Countries may barter agents one for another after a decent interval, but when murder is involved the system withers. And now, of course, you have the job of tidying up.'

Thane nodded. Far down the Falls Way, the lights of a car were heading towards them. The tidying up, as Koltsov said, was about to begin.

★ ★ ★

It was two days later before the evening flight from Inverness brought Colin Thane back to Glasgow. And the tidying up was still going on — would go on for some time.

There had been the Iron Curtain trawler reported to have landed a boat on a quiet beach near Loch Carron, a boat which had waited then gone away again, empty-handed.

There was the last stage of the Ministry's tests of the Hydrostat vehicles, postponed by the truck's destruction — though David Stanley pronounced himself prepared to bet that a contract was now certain.

There were the other loose ends, like what Stanley would do now he knew the story of John Maulden's original work on the valve gear. Like just what would emerge from the fact that Ian Shaw showed no sign of wanting to return to Canada unless Jane Maulden was equally interested.

The passenger steps clamped against the aircraft's side, its door opened, and warm, familiar Glasgow voices sounded from outside on the runway. As he gathered his hand luggage and watched Phil Moss limp with a stick towards the exit, Thane thought briefly and still wonderingly of Commander Allowes.

The Admiralty security man had taken over completely from the moment he'd arrived at the Falls Way. Only Alexis Koltsov had posed a problem, and a long telephone conversation to London had decided that for him.

'We get him patched up and invite him to take a plane back home for convalescence,' said Allowes when he'd hung up. 'The old sacred cow of diplomatic immunity, and no act of direct violence to his credit.'

'Isn't there?' Thane had asked.

Allowes had shrugged. 'Don't be awkward. We don't need one of theirs right now, but you never know the moment when we'll need some sort of credit to account. We play ball with them, they play ball with us. Call it a business arrangement.' He'd frowned and corrected himself. 'A living arrangement.'

Thane reached the foot of the aircraft steps and took a deep breath of the harsh, soot-tinged city air. There were some people waiting at the arrival gate. One of them was a middle-aged woman, small and plump, neat in a slightly old-fashioned fur coat and matching hat.

As Phil Moss reached the barrier he saw her and stopped, vaguely apprehensive. Then Emma Robertson had bustled forward, a smile on her face, going through all the actions of a mother hen whose favourite chick was returning to the nest.

Colin Thane grinned and strode over to join them. One living arrangement, at least, now seemed firmly under control.

THE END

THE INTERFACE MAN
LEAVE IT TO THE HANGMAN
BLUEBACK
WITCHROCK
LIVE BAIT
DEVILWEED
DRAW BATONS!
PILOT ERROR
THE TALLYMAN
LAKE OF FURY
AN INCIDENT IN ICELAND
PLACE OF MISTS
SALVAGE JOB
A BURIAL IN PORTUGAL
A PAY-OFF IN SWITZERLAND
CARGO RISK
ISLE OF DRAGONS
NEST OF VULTURES
THE COUNTERFEIT KILLERS
A CUT IN DIAMONDS
MAYDAY IN MALAGA
DRUM OF POWER
A PROBLEM IN PRAGUE
CAVE OF BATS
BLOOD PROOF
BLOODTIDE
WITCHLINE
DEATH BYTES
THE LAZARUS WIDOW

We do hope that you have enjoyed reading this large print book.

Did you know that all of our titles are available for purchase?

We publish a wide range of high quality large print books including:
Romances, Mysteries, Classics
General Fiction
Non Fiction and Westerns

Special interest titles available in large print are:
The Little Oxford Dictionary
Music Book
Song Book
Hymn Book
Service Book

Also available from us courtesy of Oxford University Press:
Young Readers' Dictionary
(large print edition)
Young Readers' Thesaurus
(large print edition)

For further information or a free brochure, please contact us at:
Ulverscroft Large Print Books Ltd.,
The Green, Bradgate Road, Anstey,
Leicester, LE7 7FU, England.
Tel: (00 44) 0116 236 4325
Fax: (00 44) 0116 234 0205

THE UNSETTLED ACCOUNT

Eugenia Huntingdon

As the wife of a Polish officer, Eugenia Huntingdon's life was filled with the luxuries of silks, perfumes and jewels. It was also filled with love and happiness. Nothing could have prepared her for the hardships of transportation across Soviet Russia — crammed into a cattle wagon with fifty or so other people in bitterly cold conditions — to the barren isolation of Kazakhstan. Many did not survive the journey; many did not live to see their homeland again. In this moving documentary, Eugenia Huntingdon recalls the harrowing years of her wartime exile.

FIREBALL

Bob Langley

Twenty-seven years ago: the rogue shoot-down of a Soviet spacecraft on a supersecret mission. Now: the SUCHKO 17 suddenly comes back to life three thousand feet beneath the Antarctic ice cap — with terrifying implications for the entire world. The discovery triggers a dark conspiracy that reaches from the depths of the sea to the edge of space — on a satellite with nuclear capabilities. One man and one woman must find the elusive mastermind of a plot with sinister roots in the American military elite, and bring the world back from the edge . . .

STANDING IN THE SHADOWS

Michelle Spring

Laura Principal is repelled but fascinated as she investigates the case of an eleven-year-old boy who has murdered his foster mother. It is not the sort of crime one would expect in Cambridge. The child, Daryll, has confessed to the brutal killing; now his elder brother wants to find out what has turned him into a ruthless killer. Laura confronts an investigation which is increasingly tainted with violence. And that's not all. Someone with an interest in the foster mother's murder is standing in the shadows, watching her every move . . .

NORMANDY SUMMER/
LOVE'S CHARADE

Joy St.Clair

NORMANDY SUMMER — Three cousins, Helen, Tally and Rosie, joined the First Aid Nursing Yeomanry. Helen had driven ambulances through The Blitz, but it was the Summer of 1944 that would change their lives irrevocably.

LOVE'S CHARADE — A broken down car, a mix-up of addresses and soon Kimberley found she was stand-in fiancée for a man she hardly knew. What chance had the pair of them of surviving this masquerade?

THE WESTON WOMEN

Grace Thompson

Wales, 1950s: At the head of the wealthy Weston family are Arfon and Gladys, owners of a once-successful wallpaper and paint store. It had always been Gladys's dream to form a dynasty. Her twin daughters, however, had no interest, and her grandson Jack had little ambition. And so, it is on her twin granddaughters, Joan and Megan, that Gladys pins her hopes. But unbeknown to her, they are considered rather outrageous — and one of them is secretly dating Viv Lewis, who works for the Westons but is not allowed to mix with the family socially. However, it is on him they will depend to help save the business.

TIME AFTER TIME
AND OTHER STORIES

Mary Williams

In this collection of mysterious short stories the recurring theme of 'time after time' is reflected upon with varying intensity, and in several as a haunting reminder of life's immortality. Time itself has little meaning in the wheel of eternity, and it is more than possible that the vital spark or soul of any human being could by chance contact that of another known to him or her in a previous existence on earth. Some stories concentrate on the effect of wandering apparitions about the ether and in all of them can be found love, tragedy, emotional yearnings and sheer terror.